THE RAGGED ARSED MILITIA BOY

by

BETTE VICKERS

as serialised by
BBC Radio Humberside

HUTTON PRESS
1989

Published by the Hutton Press Ltd.
130 Canada Drive, Cherry Burton, Beverley
North Humberside, HU17 7SB

Front cover design by
John Reveley.

Printed and Bound by

Clifford Ward & Co. (Bridlington) Ltd.
55 West Street, Bridlington, East Yorkshire
YO15 3DZ

ISBN 0 907033 92 X

CHAPTER 1

Young Rob Clamp grudgingly allowed himself to be propelled through the tiny wooden school gate by his sister Mary. Perhaps it would be more truthful to say he was forced to let Mary take him into the yard, for she had him firmly by the scruff of his coarse woollen shirt and was dragging him along so fast that his boot nails were firing sparks as they slid along the cobbled path.

"You little varmint, you'll be the death of me. But you ain't getting away this time. You've not been in school more than an hour all week and you've got me lying away to Mother. I'm not having it." She loosened her hold and looked down at him sighing, "What do you want to do it for, aye? And where the devil do you get to, that's what I'd like to know?"

Rob shrugged away from her and smiled shyly. "Well, if Master hadn't let on, nobody would have been any the wiser. And what do it matter anyway? What's the good of schooling?"

He grinned, knowing that Mary had a soft spot for her young brother. She didn't like school either. It was a waste of time when she could be of more use in helping Mother. But Mary didn't have Rob's nerve.

Rob was tall for his age, not handsome but attractive in a lean, bony way. Being the middle child of nineteen children, he was left very much in the care of the older girls, in particular Mary, who was relied upon to do a great many of the household tasks in the little cottage that now housed thirteen of the Clamp children in the tiny Suffolk village of Maudlesham.

He smiled at her again, but she was getting to the end of her tether and, with a great shove, she pushed him through into the boys' playground. He stood for a moment and took stock. The boys' area was divided from the babies and girls' class by a high brick wall topped with three lines of barbed wire. "Now what's the good of that?" he mused. The old gate hadn't closed properly for years and his lean body coud squeeze through the gap like greased lightning. But the wall had always been a challenge to the village lads who would try and climb over to play Kiss Catch with the girls. Many a lad had been caught on the vicious wire barbs and hung by a thread as they struggled to free themselves. Scratched and scrawked they would try to stem the tears as they ran to the pump to wash the blood away.

Fatty Walls, a big bouncy lad with a yearning for Maggie Wilson, was one whom Rob had helped to pull down and his legs and knees were so badly cut that they had to carry him across to the Master's house. It took three lads to lift him and Rob smiled as he pictured Fatty's wobbling body being manhandled across the yard. Rob had run across and slung him over one shoulder. "A fireman's carry," cheered the lads and lasses and to add to the merriment Rob and Fatty loudly sang "Here I be, here I buggery, here I come from Fareham, my old woman got plenty like me, she knows how to rear 'em." The words were emphasised by the clickety-clack of hob nailed boots as the crowd of children followed behind with a marching dance. Their young voices rang through the streets and villagers laughed and joined in the signing of the old folk song.

Now Mary turned and wagged a finger accusingly at him. "Mind you stay put," she warned. But that was up to providence for if Rob wanted to scarper then he would, and the devil take the hindmost. He would be gone like a shot, over the rolling meadows to his favourite spot in the old hollow oak tree by the lake. Sometimes she had caught a glimpse as he had escaped, moving with the swiftness and beauty of a greyhound and gone like a fleeting shadow.

The oak by the lake was a vantage spot set in a rolling meadow on a slight incline. Rob could see a hundred things at once from there. He could see the school, hear the bell and go scarpering back in time for play and a dinner of big chunks of home made bread lathered with brown beef dripping and a long cool drink from the school pump. After a play around with the lads he would run back to his hideout for the afternoon.

Rob loved the Suffolk countryside and from his panoramic view he would watch fascinated as the birds and wild life scurried and hunted. Sometimes there were courting couples and their antics made him chuckle. Sometimes there would be farmers and the men at work and Rob savoured each moment but kept it all to himself. This was his private life.

He sniggered as he remembered the day he saw the Squire's son with his sister Daisy down by Waterman's Piece. They thought they were unseen behind the great wheel mill, but not from Rob. When Daisy next went home he stared hard into her face and smirked.

"What are you looking at me like that for, you cheeky little devil?" she snapped.

Rob shrugged his shoulders and laughed at her red cheeks. Daisy was in service up at the manor. She was a pretty lass, buxom and well shaped and her rosy cheeks and delightful smile brought her many friends. She appeared to get on well in her job, especially with the Squire's son. And being in service did have its good points. Often she would bring leftover food home from the manor. It was very welcome in the Clamp house. Mother had very little money and if any cash did come in, invariably Father would drink it all into oblivion.

The Master's voice broke into his reverie. "Clamp, get yourself in here. You are not going to slide off again, my boy, not this time."

Dutifully Rob took his place in the line and then, under the Master's eagle eye, was unceremoniously dumped in the front desk in full view of teacher and pupils.

"You are like Houdini, here one minute and gone the next." The Master spoke more softly. Rob had a way with him that could melt almost anyone, anyone except his Mother when she was really angry. John Cobbolt, the headmaster of Maudlesham village school sighed. The lad didn't have much of a life in that cottage with a father who drank too much, too many children and very little money. He wondered how Mrs. Clamp managed to exist. As far as he knew, the Clamps were self employed with very little visible means of support. They swept chimneys and had a good line in logs and game. The whole family would turn out if a tree had to be felled. Even the mother would be there chopping and sawing until every bit was carted away.

But nobody really knew how they managed. Maria Clamp had never in all her married life paid for meat, vegetables, fruit or fuel. Somehow, by the Grace of God she would say, it was all provided. She earned a bit here and there as the village midwife, layer out of the dead and general sick helper. Old Tham spent the weekends in a drunken stupor, mainly from his home brews if money was short.

The villagers were very wary of Tham's hospitality and, if possible, would refuse the offer of a "Good drop of rhubarb or dandelion." Rob had tasted the home brew and enjoyed the after effects. "That blackberry is good, Father", he would say, "Good and strong with a good head, like a man should be, like you are." The old man would smile at the glib tongue of his middle son as he looked up at him with eyes so steely blue they could at times cut right through you.

The Clamps lived a rural life with home baked bread and jam in the morning swilled down with warm milk from old Dolly the cow they kept in the back field. There was bread and dripping for school dinner and then a hot meal at night made from pheasant, rabbit, or hare, potatoes and herb dumplings. Mother always made a herb dumpling and a sweet dumpling. Both were wrapped in white linen and cooked in the fire copper in the washhouse. She boiled everything, the meat and the fruit, all wrapped in separate cloths or dishes and put into the old copper to produce great mounds of white cloud that melted in your mouth, sometimes sweetened with honey from the back garden.

Rob licked his lips at the thought of this good food, and then realised that the Master was not looking. He saw his chance and like a streak of lightning he was out, through the door, round the wall and across the fields. He reached the lake, heaving great billows of breath from the deep cavern under his breast bone. Bending down, he cupped his hands and gulped great mouthfuls of water. His breathing eased and he looked up at the tree, gnarled black wrinkled bark covering its trunk with swirls of knots looking a bit like Father's ageing face. But he was here, safe from the world and he wriggled his bony body inside the hollow trunk until he could look through the hole which had once borne a branch. He settled himself down and stared before him. The world was now in view.

Across the skyline he could see smoke curling into the sky from the big factories in Bury St. Edmonds or Ipswich. Rob had never been to a town, he had never been further than Sawsden, the next village, but he had heard all about such places from his father and elder brothers. He tried to imagine what it would be like in a big town, the noise, the smoke, the twinkling lights like the Christmas tree in church, and lots of people. One day he would go. When he left school he would set off and find work in the town and earn a lot of money. He realised that that day wouldn't be far off and then he would be free of the Master and the restrictions of school.

He daydreamed of the things he might do. Work on a farm? No, he didn't fancy that. Go into service and be a skivvy? No, he wasn't the type to touch his forelock to any man. Maybe he would go on the railways or the roads with the big Irish navvys Father was always on about.

He remembered the night Father brought home big Jim McInarry, both of them drunk as lords and singing away. Hidden beneath the old horsehair sofa with hands tucked underneath his backside to keep away the striking cold of the flagstone floor, Rob had listened and chuckled at the stories and the songs, songs of Ireland and London, and of something called the seaside.

"Aye begorra, just see the soldiers of the Queen, Tham, strutting up and down outside the palace like fine peacocks."

Rob tried to picture the scene, but the only soldier he had seen had been Billy Cobier home on leave from India and he didn't look much like a peacock.

"Some ride on horses black as jet with manes all dressed and sheep lined saddles on their backs. 'Tis true, Tham, true as I'm sat here."

More like lying here, thought Rob, but he thrilled at the talk of horses. He loved horses and tried to imagine them in all their finery. It was a far cry from the old shires and brown hunters which he saw around the village. These thoughts led him to a light slumber which was rudely shattered by the voice of his father with the Master.

"Git yourself out of there boy, or I'll hide you within an inch of your dalled life."

Father was always as good as his word, but Rob stayed still knowing that they could not see him and were only guessing.

"You sure he's here, Mary?"

So that was it. Mary had told them where he was. His thoughts were abruptly halted when a bundle of smoking straw was pushed into the hollow tree. It was an old trick that his father often used to smoke lads up the great hall chimneys. The straw was damp and smokey and Rob held his breath until he felt his lungs bursting.

"You old devil," he screamed, and pushing and shoving he jumped out of the tree. Tears streaming down his cheeks and face blackened with smoke, he stood facing Mary, Father and the Master. He looked at his sister. "You rotten little ...."

With a swift crack of his whip across Rob's cheek, Father stopped the flow of abuse. "That's enough boy," he shouted.

"Don't whip the boy, Clamp, there's no need for that," the Master cried and stepped forward to stop the rain of blows. He had never got used to these rural methods of correction. Canings were all very well, but whippings, that was something not to be tolerated.

"Don't you bother yourself about that Master, I've got a much better job for this varmint than a whipping."

Rob looked up at him. Now what was the old devil up to? "You may well look, my boy. I'm going to send you to work. No more school, being as you hate it so much. You are going to work." Rob's face broke into a wide grin. He had won.

"You must have a position for him, Clamp. The boy can't leave unless he has a position," the Master said firmly.

"Oh aye, I've got that all right. He can be a chimney boy."

Rob's face fell. A chimney boy. That meant being shoved up all the awkward chimneys, naked and greased so that you could pull the brush behind you. If you got stuck they put burning straw up the chimney. That was guaranteed to get you moving. Rob had done the job once and remembered the pain of scrubbed knees and elbows from narrow turnings and loose bricks in chimneys that made it a treacherous and dangerous job. He trembled with fear. "Oh, not that Father. I'll go back to school and I'll not play truant again. I'll work at night and the weekend. I'll go to church, I will Father, I promise," he cried.

"Aye, like you promised afore? You'll be a soot boy and like it. We are up at the manor tomorrow. That will break you in." And Father turned on his heel and marched off across the meadow.

Rob ran home to Mother with Father's harsh words ringing in his ears. "I don't want to do it, Mother, please don't let me do that. I'm far too big and I'll get stuck. I won't live long if you make me," he cried.

Mother's voice was soft but unrelenting. "Now come on lovey, Father won't let you come to no harm. Buck up and after dinner go off and enjoy yourself round the village. You'll not get another chance for a long time now." His heart sank. "Here, take some lardy cake and cheese and here's a mite of cinder toffee to chew."

Rob took the things and paused at the door. "Mother, you know that shilling I earned bush beating last week and you saved it for me, can I have it now? I'll get some thick socks and a neckerchief to wear, like Father's."

Mother smiled and from the old pewter pot took out the precious coin. "Now, don't you go wasting it, and don't be late back. You'll have an early start in the morning."

Marching determinedly through the village, Rob reached the crossroads with the big white signposts. Carefully he read out the words as best he could — Lavenham, Ipswich, Bury St. Edmunds. Ipswich, that was the place. He would head for Ipswich.

Whistling tunelessly, he set off along the strange road, a road that would lead to many adventures, great adventures, he was sure of that. And anything, anything was better than being a soot boy.

CHAPTER 2

The die was cast, and having made the decision Rob marched off singing and whistling to the rhythm of his footsteps. He did a little skip and hop, swung the white linen that held his food and surged forward, never taking his eyes off the road.

Ipswich, it sounded like paradise. He reached a wide bend in the road leading over a crossroads. Carefully he read the signpost. Ipswich, he was on the right road, but now he was beginning to feel hungry and thirsty. He jumped over the grass verge and reaching down into the clear filled dyke, took off his cap, lay down and drank long and loudly from his cupped hands before swilling down his dust covered face.

"Might as well have a break now," he muttered and sitting down he leant his back against the signpost and unwrapped his food. Oh, it tasted so good, and for a moment he almost wished that he was back at home. But the thought of the manor and the great chimneys soon killed any nostalgia. It was far better to be going to Ipswich.

Rob decided to be sensible and leave a bit of food in case the journey took longer than expected, and wrapping up carefully what was left, he set off again with the same determined steps.

Looking round he could see that the fields were deserted with not a soul in sight. Come to think of it, Rob hadn't seen anyone since leaving home. It must be getting night, he thought. It was still springtime and work finished at five, just before dark. His mother would be dishing up the dinner. Rob breathed in and felt his nostrils tremble. He could almost smell the pudding.

He started to sing and dance again and felt a bit of a fool as he looked up and saw four wagons full of hay being pulled by lovely Suffolk shires. He stopped and saluted in greeting.

"Hello, young fellow-me-lad. Where are you off to then?" the lead waggoner asked.

"I'm off to ...." Now Rob had to think fast. He didn't want to be caught like this. "I'm off to see my sister in Ipswich. She's about to be confined and Mother wants to know how things are." He surprised himself with this good story, for he was not a lad of many words or imagination.

"Oh, aye. Well, best o' luck to you then, and take care. There's some right funny folk about at night."

Night? Rob hadn't thought about night. Night was dark and cold.

Night was sleeping four in a bed, head to toe and huddled together to keep warm. He felt and saw that the sun had gone down and shadows were casting across the sky bringing in the darkness. He felt scared. The shadows on the trees made funny shapes as they swayed in the light breeze and the noise was whispering and haunting.

He hurried his footsteps, but even the sound of his own feet clattering away on the road sent his hair creeping up on the back of his neck. Bravely he whistled again and then, in the far distance, he saw twinkling lights. This must be Ipswich. He broke into a run and then a gallop until he slid to a halt outside the first gas lit building. It was a pub, *The Case is Altered*, a Tolly Cobbold Inn, full to overflowing with laughter, singing and raised voices.

At first, he was startled and afraid, but they all seemed to be enjoying themselves. Dare he go in? Yes, Rob Clamp dare do anything. Pulling himself up to his full height so that nobody would question his age, he gingerly pushed open the swing doors.

What a place it was. What a sight of men and women, some lolling in their seats, some women sat on men's knees, others staggering, singing or trying to dance. "A den of iniquity", he could almost hear the Parson's voice ringing out from the pulpit.

"Yes?" a brusque voice interrupted his gaze.

"Errr-err.."

"Come on lad, I ain't got all night. What do you want?"

"A pint of Mother's milk, by the look of him," a voice boomed out from the crowd.

Rob looked up and met the gaze of the tallest man he had ever seen, and that took in his brother George who stood at least six feet four. But the man looked kindly and had a bright twinkle in his dark brown eyes.

"Evening, sir." Rob touched his cap as Mother would wish him to do.

"Evening, son. Well-mannered lad and all. What brings you here? You don't look old enough to be out on your own let alone in a place like this?"

"I'm to visit my sister. Mother wants to know how things are since she's to be confined shortly." The story rolled off his tongue so well he could see that the man was taken in.

"Where does she live then?"

Now that was a different matter. Rob had no idea of roads or names. "I know the place, sir, but not the name. Not too good at reading. It's Lavenham way somewhere."

"That's miles away yet lad. Here, I reckon you'd best come long home with me for the night. My missus will give you a bed and a bite to eat."

Rob wasn't sure about this. He was not really a dishonest lad and felt guilty about accepting hospitality taken on a lie. "That's all right, sir. I've got friends up the road and they'll be expecting me."

"What made you stop here then?"

Rob hardly knew what to say and didn't want to add to the lies. "I was dry, sir, and couldn't go on another step." Now Rob was brusque and, with a nod to the landlord, ordered half a pint of mixed, remembered words from his father and brothers.

"It's pints," and without more ado a pint pot of foam-headed brown velvet was placed before him.

Rob proffered the shilling and was given eleven pence change. The pint was a bit overpowering and he didn't really have any notion what to do with it. He could feel the eyes of the tall man boring into his neck and so, with a sweeping flourish, he picked up the drink and took a long gulp. "That was good. Hit the right spot first time." Rob tried to smile and then almost choked as the bitter liquid hit his stomach and made him retch.

"You were ready for that lad. Like a drop or two do we?" The tall man stood with his hands on his hips surveying Rob's reactions.

"Now and again. Father brews at home and we often share a glass." Well at least that was the truth. Rob was careful to take more time over the rest of the drink and finished off with a piece of lardy cake and cheese from his cloth.

"Your mother sent you prepared then?"

"Aye, she's a good 'un and no mistake." He felt sad at the thought of home. Would they have missed him yet? He was so often out in the fields at night they might think he had gone off in a paddy because of his father's actions. Oh, he would give anything to see his mother's smile as she handed him his mug of hot milk. His stomach lurched at the thought of the milk and he sighed again. "I'd best be off then. I don't want to keep people waiting up for me."

"Here, have another one boy." A younger man watching from the corner approached and offered Rob a drink.

"You get along now boy" the landlord interrupted.

Rob sensed that a warning was being given and, picking up the cloth that held his food, he left by the side door. The cool night air struck his face and made him catch his breath. The moonlight spread a beam along the long cobbled street that was now deserted and only the sound of the remaining pub revellers broke the silence. Which way to turn? He gelt giddy, sick, and tired from too long without real food in his belly and the effects of the drink. He leaned against a hissing gas lamp and wiped his forehead. The thought of the manor's chimney didn't seem half so daunting as he stood alone in this strange town. He sighed in the stillness and then, with a sudden burst, it seemed that all the world had entered the street. The pub was closing.

Gathering his wits, he quickly ran to the end of the road and found himself confronted by a yard full of corrugated sheds. There was a sudden rattle, pounding and shaking of the ground and with a thunderous noise a train rushed past. Rob had never heard or seen a train before and in his excitement he tried to climb over the heaps of coal in the engine yard. The engine huffed and puffed and sparks hissed and flew out of the boiler as it sped by.

After all this excitement Rob felt revived and ready to go on again. Under one of the sheds a fire burned in a basket sending out a warm and welcoming glow. Rob made towards it. Several men sat round, hands outstretched to the red embers. They look up, unshaven and ragged, eyes red rimmed and heavy.

"Evening then." He tried to speak with confidence. The reply was a grunt. He took a closer look and the stench of bodies, damp and unwashed, steaming in the heat of the fire, made him back off. They were tramps, vagabonds.

"What you want then?" One man tried to stand. He lurched forward, as he tried to take a drink from a bottle of vile looking purple liquid.

"Just a warm afore I go to my mates."

"Sit down then. Got a drink?" Rob shook his head. "Anything to eat?" Rob offered what was left in the cloth and they fell on it like rats.

He was so tired his eyes were closing in spite of desperately trying to keep awake. He didn't feel safe here, but where could he go? This Ipswich was not the glittering town he had been led to believe. "Settle down here, on this newspaper. It'll keep you warm." Rob was a little reassured. Maybe they weren't so bad after all. Gratefully he settled into an uneasy slumber.

His awakening was abrupt. Two men were set upon him and

roughly and crudely taking off his clothes. His boots and socks had already gone and as the freezing air hit his body, he realised they were taking off his trousers and shirt. Fear and terror gripped his young heart and his body went rigid with fright.

"Ger off, you thieving buggers, ger off." Valiantly he fought with feet, fists and teeth, but these seasoned men were too strong.

He was nearly naked when a voice rang out with authority, "Leave the boy be. Clear off, all of you. Leave his things or I'll have your guts for garters and feed them to the dogs."

The men fell away and Rob tried to cover his nakedness before looking up into the eyes of the tall man. His lips trembled and for a horrifying minute Rob thought he was going to blubber. He bit his lip and began to dress.

"Now then, my boy, what's your game, the truth mind you."

Rob trembled and thought of father. He wasn't going to be afraid. Rob Clamp feared neither man nor beast. "If it's any of your business, I ain't got no game. What's it got to do with you anyway?" At first his voice shook, but as he spoke it grew stronger and more angry.

"Well, I'll just show you what it's got to do with me," and he grabbed Rob by the shoulder and propelled him through the street.

"Are you the police then?"

"Sort of. You'll find out."

Now he had gone and done it. They'd make him go back home to face father and the whipping of his life. They might even lock him up for the night. At this thought he could not stop the fear and the tears began to fall. He shook from terror and cold and grabbing the man's hand he began to beg, "Don't let them lock me up mister. I ain't done no wrong. Let me go and I'll not be any bother." Every word was spoken in fear.

The man looked down and Rob's heart sank as he saw the look in his eyes. He was finished. He was going to end up a gaol bird on the first night. He wished he had never heard of Ipswich, and as for adventures, to hell with them.

Suddenly, the manor chimneys, with all their nooks and crannies, were very inviting.

CHAPTER 3

As he was propelled along the street, Rob could feel the firm grip of the man's hand pressing into his shoulder. It felt as if he was about to be dragged through the town, but after turning down a side passage that led into a courtyard, he opened a brown painted front door and they entered a room that was brightly lit by two gas burners placed on each side of the chimney breast.

"Now look what I have brought home missus," the man said.

From behind the spindles of a high backed chair at the corner of the fireplace a woman raised herself up and looked over the top at Rob. "Goodness me, what's this then?" she asked and getting up quickly came round the chair to face the unlikely duo.

"It's a young lad, barely out of nappies. He's been giving me some cock and bull tale about seeing his sister and some friends. I reckon he's a runaway."

Rob shuffled his feet and looked down at the pegged rug that covered the cocoa matting on the floor.

The woman laughed at his forlorn face. "What if he has? It's no more than you did at his age," she said.

"Aye, well, maybe, but now we've got to have some home truths. Come on, lad. What's your name for a start?"

"Rob, sir, Rob Clamp. I'm from Maudlesham and I ran off 'cos they was making me a soot boy." The words and some of the story came tumbling out.

"Hmm. Well, first, I ain't sir, I'm sergeant, Sergeant Wilberforce Craddock of Her Majesty's Coldstream Guards. And this 'ere is my lady wife, Mrs. Craddock."

Rob realised then why the man had seemed so much in command, why he held himself so upright and tall and his voice held so much authority. He was a soldier.

"Why ain't you in uniform then?" Rob questioned.

"Because I've been giving it a good brush and clean up, that's why."

"The sergeant is on a recruiting campaign, looking for likely lads to join the colours." Mrs. Craddock emphasised the words and smiled proudly up at her husband. She too was tall and thin, but with a kindly face. She was quite pretty really, with her dark brown hair taken over her face in waves and then coiled into the nape of her neck.

"That's enough of that, my dear. Let's get this lad fed and then washed and abed. We'll talk in the morning." And without more ado the kettle was slung on the hob, water poured into a large flowered tea pot, bread cut and spread with butter and jam and a large piece of cake taken from a tin and placed on the side of the plate topped with a good lump of cheddar cheese. It was a feast.

Rob sat at the table and between mouthfuls of food and gulps of tea tried to tell them as little as possible and yet give the impression that he was giving his life story. This time he didn't lie, not outright, but he did leave a lot out such as the bits about school and seeing things he 'didn't ought'. But he belaboured the point about being a soot boy and made to go to work.

"What a cruel thing to do and no mistake. A fine young lad like you should make summat more on hissen than a soot boy," Mrs. Craddock tut-tutted and patted his shoulder. Rob warmed to her kindness.

"How old are lad?" asked the sergeant.

Rob paused before answering, intent on chewing the last morsel of cake and at the same time allowing himself time to think. If he told his real age they would send him back home and inform the police, as his father had often said he would do when any of his brothers had threatened to run away. He decided to play safe. "Nearly sixteen sir, er sergeant, nearly sixteen." He looked at the sergeant and breathed with relief as he saw him accept his age without question.

"You're a fine lad, no doubt about that, and you've got a bit of spirit. We'll have to see what we can do for you. Get them clothes off now and into the tub."

Rob stared in amazement as Mrs. Craddock dragged in a wooden washtub and placed it on a thick layer of newspapers on the rug in front of the fire. The side boiler was emptied into the tub. Steaming ladles of water filled the tub right to the soap shelf. A bar of green Sunlight soap was thrown in followed by a flannel and big white square towels were hung over a clothes horse set behind the tub to give him privacy. Rob had never seen anything like it in his life.

"Get on now, clothes off and into this tub. It's high time you were in bed and you ain't going between my sheets until some of that muck is off," said Mrs. Craddock.

"I can't ... I ain't ..." The words were stopped as the sergeant grabbed his arm and with a few deft pulls and tugs had him undressed, all but his socks and boots. He looked such a sight, hands carefully poised in front of his privates to hide his modesty and naked except for thick woollen socks that had now dropped to his ankles and were resting on top of black hob nailed boots.

"Come on lad, get in there." The sergeant laughed and Rob bent over carefully and took off his boots and socks before sinking into the warm embrace of the water.

He leaned back and resting his head on the back of the tub allowed the warm sensuous feeling to run through his body. He had almost fallen asleep when the sergeant peered round the makeshift screen and shouted, "Come on, we ain't got all night." His reverie was broken and he jumped out quickly and rubbed himself down with soft white towels. "Get this shirt on. It's a mite big, but it'll keep your backside warm. Do his hair, Mother. There now, let's take a look." The screen was taken down and the sergeant picked up the still steaming tub and threw the contents through the door into the yard. Rob felt a little uneasy as if he was being inspected for more than just being tucked up in bed. "Hmm, tall, bit scraggy, but you'll fill out nicely with the raising. Not bad looking and could be soon smartened up. We'll see, we'll see."

By this time Rob was far too tired to wonder what he meant, and meekly followed Mrs. Craddock up the turning stairs into a candlelit room. It seemed tiny, but the light was so dim Rob couldn't make anything out. He saw the bed with the sheets turned back. Sheets, not hessian, and not coats on the bed but a patchwork quilt that was bright and clean. Heaving a great sigh he lay down and only vaguely remembered the covers being tucked around him before he fell into a deep dreamless sleep. It had been quite a day.

He slept soundly until the sergeant woke him with a gentle shaking. "That's it, lad, show a leg. Breakfast is on the table. Have a swill in the bowl there and get down afore it wastes."

Rob looked round the room. Daylight was streaming in through the tiny window and resting on the big rose pink jug and bowl on the washstand beneath the windowsill. The door was slightly open and from down the stairs there wafted the most delicious smell of bacon, fried bacon. For a moment he thought of home and Mother. Would she be worrying, would Father be angry, would the police be set on to look for him? Hunger delayed further fears and, quick as a flash, he swilled himself down and went downstairs still in his woollen nightshirt.

"You too hungry to get dressed then?" Mrs. Craddock asked as

Rob folded the tail of the shirt round his backside and sat down at the table in front of a plate of eggs, bacon and fried bread.

"Couldn't find my clothes, misses." He smiled and looked as she pointed to a neat pile of clothes that were his. They had been washed, ironed and folded all ready to wear. If this was how Ipswich folk lived there must be some money about and the sooner he looked for a job the better, he thought to himself.

"Now, get dressed and comb that hair. Mrs. Craddock handed him a piece of broken tortoiseshell comb which he pulled through his hair and smoothed down with water from the ladle. "You keep that, lad, keep yourself tidy."

He tucked the piece of comb in his trouser pocket and sat and watched as the sergeant got dressed in his bright red tunic with the shining brass buttons in measured lengths down the front. His dark blue trousers had a knife-edged crease in them and when he put on his pillbox hat, he looked a real toff.

"You want to come along?" he asked, and Rob nodded eagerly. Mrs. Craddock handed her husband his stick and after proudly rubbing the gold stripes on his sleeve, gave him a resounding kiss.

Rob felt proud to be with this man who cut such a fine figure that people turned to look at him as he strode along the street. "Come on, lad, let's show you a bit of life. Walk tall and straight. Put your shoulders back and step our smartly. Rob did as he was ordered and they swung down the road together, in perfect step, although Rob had to stride to keep up.

The noise and sights fascinated Rob: the roll of cartwheels on the road, horses clattering along with a sing-song rhythm, people and voices. There were thousands of people and shops that sold everything. There was food he had never seen before and so many pubs he wondered how they all made a living. Drunks lumbered about all over in spite of it being early morning and kids stood on the pavement outside begging and pickpocketing from them as they came out of the pubs. He watched as a barefoot lad held out his hand piteously to receive a few pence.

The sergeant called into the pub and Rob thought he might try begging. He hadn't much money left and he might not get such good lodgings tonight. He doffed his cap and was about to receive a coin when a large hand caught him a clip behind the ear. "No begging, lad. You should be too proud for that. Work for a living and earn your bread." Rob silently agreed. Work, he would have to find a job and be quick about it.

They walked towards a group of lads who were larking about around the street corner. They began to shout and jeer at the sergeant. "Watch out, here he comes, Soldier of the Queen. The Colonel himself no doubt. Got your buttons cleaned have we? See your arse in your boots can we?"

The insults came thick and fast, but the sergeant appeared to ignore them and strode along until they were almost past the last man and then, like a snarling dog, he whipped round and lashed several of them with his stick. Rob thought they were in for a real old do and without thinking he waded in with boots and fists and having been taught to stick up for himself, gave a good account. The battle was short-lived. The enemy was no match for Rob and the sergeant and they ran like scared rabbits along the road.

"Not so tough now, are we my lads, not now you've met your match," Rob delighted in shouting after them.

The sergeant stopped him abruptly. "Don't gloat lad, victory is enough." And again in silence they marched off. "You did well there lad. Lost your rag a bit did we?"

Rob shook his head. "No, I don't reckon so. Just felt it were right thing to do," he muttered. His reward was a pat on the shoulder.

By now they had reached the barracks. When they approached the gate the guards drew to attention as the sergeant entered. Rob stared. The sergeant was being treated like a king!

The barracks were built around a huge square on which groups of soldiers were marching, running, jumping and exercising. The sergeant pointed with his stick, saying, "Exercise lad, that's the thing. Keeps you fit in mind and body."

Fascinated, Rob watched and did not realise the sergeant had gone until he came out onto the square in vest and long black cotton pants. He began to exercise, bending, stretching and running on the spot. Rob watched and the rhythm got hold of him and he began to imitate the movements. Arms up — down — knees bend — arms swinging — touch the floor — running on the spot bringing the knees up almost to the chin. His face was alight and he was in a world of his own. Soon he was sweating so he took off his jacket and laid it down neatly on the ground. Keeping up with the men made him sweat even more and he took off his shirt and after wiping his face and neck placed it on top of his jacket.

He looked and saw the sergeant smiling across at him. "Tell you what lad, I'll give you a race," he shouted. Rob loved running and without hesitation agreed.

A group of men surrounded them. "What's the stake then sarge, what's the odds?" they asked.

"Let's see, I'll take you three times round the square and if you win I'll give you free board and lodging for a week. If I win, I'll let you join the army. How's that?"

Rob thought for a minute. Join the army? It might not be a bad thing. "Right boss, I'm game."

"Hold on there sarge, the lad's got boots on. Here, try these," and Rob was handed a pair of soft black running shoes. They fitted like a glove and his feet had never felt anything so soft and light.

A starter was appointed and side by side they waited for the signal. "Right, ready — steady — go." They were off, neck and neck like two greyhounds around the square.

"By jingo, the lad can run," thought the sergeant, who had been prepared to give Rob a leeway for encouragement. Rob was streaking away like lightning as he used to do across the fields. This was flat hard land and he felt each tread as his foot hit the ground.

"Come on sarge, play the game. Let's see you run." Shouts from the interested sideline had brought out more soldiers from the barracks to watch this race between a seasoned army veteran and a scraggy, shabby-looking lad.

The sergeant increased his speed as best he could, but in the last lap Rob took over with ease. He was away, breathing deep with lungs almost bursting. He ran for his life and was half way round again before they stopped and told him he was the winner.

"I won?" he questioned.

"Yes, you little bugger," the sergeant spoke from the ground where he lay gasping and panting. "You little whipper-snapper, where did you learn to run like that?"

Rob just laughed and went to put on his shirt and jacket. He was being cheered and patted on the back and just for running.

"Come on then lad, you won fair and square. Free board and lodging for a week is it?"

Rob paused and looked up at the sergeant. "Can I join the army and all then sergeant?"

The sergeant pursed his lips and took a deep breath. "That's what you want then?"

"Yes." Rob's answer was firm, but not enough for the sergeant.

"You sure?"

"I'm sure mate." Rob laughed this time and the sergeant cuffed his ear and joined in the laughter.

"Tell you what, stop with me and the missus a week and come up to the barracks. Then, if you're still of the same mind, I'll be proud to enlist you. How's that for a bargain?" He held out his hand.

With a spit on the palm, Rob shook it firmly and drew himself up to attention as he had seen the other men do. " A bargain it is then sergeant."

CHAPTER 4

In years to come, when Rob was asked about his happiest memory he would answer, "The week's free board and lodging with Craddock and my first taste of army life." As far as he was concerned, it was his first taste of heaven.

Meals were served on time and the day began at half-past five with a wash followed by a cooked breakfast. At six o'clock, hair smartened down and his boots, laid out ready the night before were put on bright and shining so that his face reflected in the toecaps. Days were spent marching, physical exercises, working on the assault course, bulling up kit, reading and writing and then back to the Craddocks for an evening meal, preparation for the next day and bed. At times he was so tired he fell asleep before finishing the meal and the sergeant would carry him up to bed.

He never forgot that experience of kindness and comradeship and after only three days he was well ready to join the colours. "You'll wait until the end of the week my lad, like we arranged," Sergeant Craddock told him. "Joining up is a major step."

The day in the barracks began with a parade and salute on the square at seven sharp taken by the Colonel. Each man was closely inspected and the smartest one was given the stick which was a great honour. Many were given fatigues for some minor dress offence such as buttons not bright enough, creases not knife-edged enough or a hat too much to the side of the head.

Rob watched carefully from the side of the square, dreaming of the day when he would be amongst the ranks. He had been taken to meet the Colonel on the first day and had given a good account of himself.

"Don't be afraid lad, but be courteous and stand straight. The Colonel is a powerful man. He can block or agree to your coming into the colours," Sergeant Craddock had warned.

But he need not have bothered, for Rob doffed his cap and stood stiffly to attention with his thumbs down the sides of his trousers. The Colonel smothered a smile at Rob's eagerness and took in the lad's tall, lean build, pleasant face and determined chin. The most striking feature was the coldness of the blue eyes, with an expression that showed no fear. With training the Colonel knew that the lad would make a good soldier.

"Looks a likely lad, Sergeant Craddock. Don't know as I'd want to tackle him in a skirmish, eh?"

The sergeant smiled in agreement. If the lad turned out good, it would be a feather in his cap.

The life fitted Rob like a glove and Rob fitted the life so well he felt he was born for just that purpose. He enjoyed the training and would laugh as the others puffed around the course while he streaked ahead. He was allowed to tackle everything except the rifle range and gunnery.

He was attached to Sergeant Craddock's squad and worked with two other new platoon intakes assigned to Sergeant Tom Macey and Sergeant Jack Wilson. A certain amount of rivalry went on between them and a lot was directed towards Rob who was considered to be 'the sergeant's lad'. But Craddock gave him no quarter and Rob expected none. He was made to do all things and although by far the youngest, he kept pace with them all.

"He'll make a fine soldier, a real credit to you Craddock. Where did you find him?" the sergeant was questioned in the mess and he would relate the circumstances, with a bit of relish, of how he found Rob roaming the streets of Ipswich. He wondered about the lad's background. He was a bit rough, but with a bit of something about him that was different. He couldn't be a runaway or the police would have visited the barracks. The army was the first place they looked for lads who left home. But he never questioned and felt that Rob would volunteer the information when he was ready.

Rob thought very little about home. He was too busy practising to be a soldier. At odd times he wondered about his mother, but felt that his absence meant one mouth less to feed and one body less to look after. He considered he was doing her a favour. If his father wanted him back that much, he could have found him. He was better off here, starting a new life, and they were better off without him.

Each week the platoon points were added up and the scores compared in a friendly competition. The two with the highest scores would organise a sporting event to get an all out winner. It was healthy and good for moral and the competitive element that made young lads into soldiers.

Towards the end of Rob's week it was decided that the event would be bare fist fighting of eight rounds or the first fall. George Abbot from Macey's squad and Charlie Cook from Wilson's were chosen for the bout. Both were fine lads who had shown throughout the training course that they could handle themselves well.

Rob grew exceited. He always enjoyed a good scrap and had been highly regarded by his brothers and the village lads for his ability in weaving and landing punches. He would run towards rather than run away from a good scrap and was nearly always the victor.

On the Saturday afternoon, as the men gathered to watch the fight, the parade square filled with excitement. Abbot was a big, strong lad, with rippling muscles. Cook was smaller, stocky and thick set, but very stong and able to move. Sergeant Craddock was the referee. His squad had been placed third and he had no man taking part, a blow to his pride especially as he had set out to impress Rob with his training schemes.

Each man picked a second who crouched at the side of the makeshift ring with a bottle of cold water and a towel at the ready. "Right now lads, a fight to the finish, fair and square now. Seconds out." And the fight was on.

The men, almost bent double, faced one another with clenched fists raised and parried and hovered around one another. "Get on with it," Rob shouted and was backed by a loud cheer of "You tell 'em, young 'un."

Abbot pounced and the punching began. They twisted, ducked and dived. Noses bled, lips burst and eyes became swollen as bare, hard knuckles hit soft flesh. Rob cheered whoever appeared to be winning, changing sides as the punches landed and the men fell and got up again to the count.

"You're a clever little devil. You want to have a go then, being as your old Dad ain't got anyone in his squad good enough?" a cheerful voice shouted behind Rob.

"He ain't my father and any time you want a scrap, you're welcome," he snapped.

"You fighting for the honour of old Haddocck-face then?"

Rob flew like a broken glass and swung round to punch the soldier square on the chin. Craddock was almost God, as far as Rob was concerned.

"Why you little bugger, I'll have you for that."

"Any time," Rob answered and turned to watch the fight again.

"Challenge the little bugger, Frank, teach him a lesson, take him on," the voices jeered encouragement.

"Right, I will then. Behind the ablutions tonight at nine. I'll teach you not to be so glib my lad."

Rob laughed and nodded his head in agreement. The fight was

almost over. George Abbot landed his final punch and was acclaimed the winner. Rob cheered and ran forward to greet the victor.

"You a bit bloodthirsty lad?" Sergeant Craddock said as he barred his way.

"No, but I enjoy a good scrap."

"Well, you just scrap off then and tell the missus I'll be home in an hour when we've got this lot settled."

Rob did as he was bid and marched across the square towards the gate. As he turned the cookhouse corner he came face to face with the soldier he had challenged.

"You remember, my lad, nine o'clock, back of ablutions." He was still laughing as Rob answered, "I'll be there, don't you fret."

"And pigs will fly," came the rejoinder.

As he entered the house, Mrs. Craddock greeted him with a smile and told him to rest himself until the sergeant got home. He sat, savoured the smell of the meal to come and felt that life was good. It was Saturday, the night out on the town. After tea Sergeant and Mrs. Craddock were getting ready for the weekly treat to the music hall followed by a drink with friends at the *Last Post*. "Sets you up for the weekend," smiled Mrs. Craddock.

"You get yourself smartened up lad, go out down the town yourself," said the sergeant as he pressed a two shilling piece into Rob's hand.

Rob smiled his gratitude and rubbed the coin unbelievingly before putting it carefully into his trouser pocket.

The trio set off together, the sergeant in his best blues, his wife in a blue stiff silk dress and jacket topped by a large black hat complete with feather boa. Rob had only seen such clothes on gentry and wondered what his mother would think to it all. He had never seen her in a coat, only the old black shawl she wore when it was really cold.

Rob stared as they reached the music hall. Crowds of pople were surging through the huge double doors, all laughing and joking as the sound of the overture came trilling through.

"Why not come along inside. Ever been to a music hall?" Rob shook his head and the sergeant shepherded him through and took his place in the box office queue. He gave Rob a small pink ticket saying, "There, you get yourself off in the gods with the young 'uns and enjoy yourself."

Rob followed the crowd as directed and they pushed and shoved him good-humouredly up the stairs where he found himself sitting between two young couples on the front row of the top balcony. The seats were rough wooden forms and Rob felt he was up in the sky. The gods was the right word. He leaned forward, resting his chin on the balcony rail and had an excellent view of the stage.

The orchestra played and the music soared to the top of the brightly lit and decorated auditorium of gold on red decoration on the walls with lights that flickered. It was a magic cave to the young lad from Maudlesham who had dared to brave the big outside world.

As the music died away, the curtains opened to show a street scene full of dancing girls who kicked their legs so high Rob thought they would reach up to the roof. He laughed as they showed bright garters and silk knickers and tossed their curls as they danced in rhythm. He clapped until his arms ached, savouring every minute. *The Song Bird*, Molly St. Clare, touched the depths of his heart with her beautiful voice and the soft words of her love songs.But he loved the comedian who ended his act with rude ditties that made him laugh until the tears rolled down his cheeks.

Never had he known such pleasure, the city lights, the life, and he could see himself in his uniform with hat cocked to one side and a curly moustache. Join the army and travel, maybe go to London. The thrilling thoughts filled his mind as he joined in singing *Soldiers of the Queen* and stood to attention for the National Anthem. With a heart as high as a bird in flight and footsteps light, he went into the cold night air. There, reality hit him. The scrap. He had forgotten the scrap.

"What's the time, mister?" he asked. Eight o'clock. There was still time to keep his assignation. He roamed idly through the streets and stood staring at the advert hoardings when several voices interrupted his thoughts.

"Well, if it ain't the snapper then. You ready for that scrap lad?"

Rob turned to face his opponent standing amongst a crowd of friends. "Any time mate," he answered.

"No time like the present. Come on lad, let's get it over with round the back here." And they led him to the back of the pub into a big yard surrounded by empty casks and barrels.

"You ain't going to take this little snapper on are you? Hardly seems fair to me." It was the afternoon's victor, George Abbot, standing at the edge of the gathering.

"Don't you worry mate. I can take him with one hand tied behind my back," Rob told him.

"In that case, I'll second you then."

To all of them it was good fun, but Rob was deadly serious. "Who's holding the purse then?" someone shouted. Rob stared as the money was thrown on the floor. Johnson, his opponent, was getting the best odds. George Abbot placed a shilling on Rob for encouragement and one or two more betted a sixpence. Rob carefully placed his florin on the pile of coins and asked, "What's the odds on me?" Twenty to one he was told. "Then put that on me." The words were drowned in the laughter.

Johnson stripped to the waist, but Rob only removed his jacket. They looked an odd pair, the smart soldier playing a game and the young lad in short trousers, woollen socks and hob-nailed boots in deadly earnest. Rob wasted no time and waded in with clenched fists. Johnson ducked and dived, but Rob carefully took his measure and was soon landing heavy blows.

"By hell, the little devil means it."

The fun was over and both men fought in earnest. Rob battled like a tiger, a tiger with a plan to win. Every blow counted and hit its target. Johnson landed some heavy blows, but he was no match for Rob's swift movements. After each round he faced Abbot who wiped him down and gave him a long drink of cold beer.

"You ain't bad snapper. You keep going and I reckon you might pull it off."

They fought on. Johnson was tough and though Rob was the younger he had more experience learned from his brothers and dodging his father's blows when he got a whipping. But he was tired and thought maybe he should give in. It had been a good fight, fought fair and square. There would be no dishonour. But Johnson too was tired and he floundered and slipped as he swung round, walking right into a left hook that brought blood spouting from both nostrils and lips. "Enough," he panted and personally lifted Rob's hand to declare him the winner.

"What the hell is all this?" a stern voice shouted and three burly policemen approached.

"Nothing, constable, a friendly scrap that's all."

"Who's this one. He's not one of your lot is he?" The policeman took hold of Rob's shoulder.

"He's all right, constable. He's my lad." Sergeant Craddock stepped forward as from nowhere to Rob's great relief and claimed him. "Get your things together and let's get home."

Rob looked at him. "What are you doing here?"

"What are you doing here is more important. What are you getting mixed up in?"

"He was defending your honour, sarge. We ragged him about you not having a contestant this afternoon and he said he'd take on any of us in your name. And he won, fair and square the lad's won." Frank Johnson, now fully dressed walked forward and offered his hand. His face was swollen, but he was smiling.

Rob shook his hand and said, "Thanks mate, I enjoyd that."

"I don't know as I did. You're all right lad. Reckoning on joining up are you?" Johnson said.

"Am I?" Rob fixed the sergeant with a stare.

"I reckon so. We'd be barmy not to take you, but I've a feeling we might live to regret it!"

Rob grinned. His future was set. Once he was in the army they couldn't take him back home. The army would be his home. He remembered the purse and, turning back, asked for his winnings. "I wagered two bob, remember?" A mixture of coins was tipped into his cap and he clutched them tightly as he marched at the side of his idol. "Fancy a drink then, sergeant. I'm treating?" His ear was cuffed and the cap taken firmly from his hand.

"You'll never have anything lad if you start them daft tricks. There must be thirty bob or more there. You take this for the paymaster to keep. It'll do nicely and give you a good start."

Rob squared his shoulders. He was a soldier — well almost, he had thirty bob in his pocket — a small fortune, and the world was at his feet.

CHAPTER 5

Rob stood in line waiting patiently for his medical examination. He watched as the doctor ordered each man to step forward and in a casual, almost uncaring way, barked "Drop 'em." It caused a bit of a laugh at first for they were clutching onto their belongings and trying to stand and look as though they had good physiques. The first lad stepped forward smartly enough, but on the order to drop them had let go of all his belongings which scattered all over the place.

The next lad stepped forward to help and, picking up a sock that was so filthy it almost stood up on its own, shouted out, "Hells bells mate, I hope you don't sleep near me. This stink's worse than our closet." It caused a riot of laughter.

"Stop this. Attention. We don't want a rabble in the army," the Medical Orderly Sergeant shouted and at once order reigned. Trousers were dropped to order and the doctor tapped here and there, said "Cough" in a mysterious voice, pulled down eyelids and sounded chests. After each one he said "A1," which meant they were fit to join the Army.

The feelng was tense as each one got nearer to the moment of truth. Most of them had come to get away from homes that were rough and poverty stricken. Some were young married men who had given up trying to find and keep down a job with enough money to support a family. They were looking for stability and maybe the chance of cheap accommodation. Others were from the criminal classes trying to hide from the law or had been given the option by magistrates of going to prison or joining the army.

For the first time since leaving home Rob questioned his own motives. He ran away to get away from his father's threat and then, as fate had turned out, things had taken a surprising turn. He had been given a taste of the army before he actually joined. He was now eager to join the colours, not really from any patriotic duty, but because he had taken to the life with an enthusiasm that even Sergeant Craddock had found surprising.

As he watched the doctor poking about the bodies of the men, he got nervous. Would they pass him? Would they tell his real age? What if they turned him down? His thoughts and doubts made him shiver. More than anything else in the world he wanted to be a soldier. He wanted to be fit, to learn a trade and be somebody, just like his adopted hero Sergeant Craddock. He unbuckled his belt as his turn came nearer and then waited for the order, "Drop 'em." Immediately he let go of his belt with no fumbling around and instantly his short trousers fell in a pathetic heap at his feet.

"What's this then, Sergeant Major? Don't get many lads in shorts."

Rob held his breath and then said in a rush of words, "Well, you see Sir, we're a poor family. I'd have got a long pair if I'd got a proper job, but with only helping my father out here and there we'd not got enough money."

But the doctor was not paying attention. He prodded and pushed Rob in the groin and said, "Cough," Rob coughed. He sounded his chest and Rob stood to his full height with shoulders well back in the hope of belying his age. "Well, you're a good sample lad. Another one A1, Sergeant Major. Good sample this lot, what? Sign here lad."

A piece of white paper was held in front of him and Rob signed as best he could with the hindrance of holding his clothes together and trying to hide his delight. He almost wept with joy and as he gathered his clothes together he did a little skip as he went towards the Medical Orderly for his jabs.

"Steady in the ranks there lad." The familiar voice of Sergeant Craddock echoed above his head. "On your way now and get kitted out." Rob looked at him with a cheeky grin and was delighted to get a conspiratorial wink in return. A fondness had grown between the two, the military man who was so regimented in his outlook and this young country lad. Even the missus had been sorry to see the lad go and had given him half a crown to take with him, "Just in case."

Rob was kitted out with underpants, 2 vests, 2 pairs of socks, shorts, shirts, boots, jacket, trousers, towel, shaving and washing kit, needles and cotton, polishing gear and brasso. He had never known such luxury or such organisation. If a garment did not fit, a tailor was brought in and in next to no time the machine was working and the alteration made. He felt like a king. But he worried about his shaving kit of mug, soap, brush and cut throat razor. He hadn't shaved yet but he made no comment and, grasping his pile of clothes neatly laid in front of him, he took his eating irons and marched proudly over to the barracks.

Private Robert Clamp 18203. Now he was somebody. He had an identification, as a solidier of the Queen. He belonged to her now and nobody could touch him.

He was shown to his bed and given his locker keys and immediately set to work polishing his boots. "Hold on a minute there lad. Not that way. Can't you bloody wait?" Rob looked up vacantly at the soldier standing at the foot of his bed.

"Stand up when I speak to you lad." Rob stood up. "To attention lad." Rob stood to attention. "I'm the training soldier lad. You're in my squad, God help me. All of you now stand to attention." The room shuffled and stood at the foot of their beds.

"To attention I said. Come on there, chests out. Legs together lad. I could drive a herd of pigs through them knees." And with his stick he prodded the unfortunate lad between the legs bringing the stick up with such force that it brought a squeal of pain.

"You needn't squeal like that lad, there's plenty more where that came from. Now pay attention. I said attention lad." He used his stick again to the back of an unfortunate pair of knees and they got the message. As one man they sprang to attention, chest out, knees together and chin well in.

"I'm a trained soldier, and when you address me you say, yes Trained Soldier, no Trained Soldier. Name is Lobbs, Private Samuel Lobbs and I'm in charge of you lot, Squad D. The Corporal is Corporal Atkins. He'll be along in a minute and he's the Corporal in Charge. And you'd better watch it 'cos he's a holy terror. He'll soon knock you into shape quicker than you can say 'Take me home Mother'. Now then, attention."

Corporal Atkins entered the barrack room. He was tall and very thin, but Rob felt this belied a fanactic fitness. Without a word he marched up and down the lines looking intently at each man, touching a neck here and there and barking, "Hair cut at least three inches off Trained Soldier." Trained Soldier barked, "Yes Corporal," in reply.

On reaching Rob he looked intently into his face. "So, this is Craddock's little boy is it?" Rob sensed hostility, but his face showed nothing. He kept his eyes focused straight in front, remembering the sergeant's instructions to hear all, see all and say nothing, like the three wise monkeys. "Well, we'll soon see what you're made of my lad." He touched Rob's soft cheek. "Bum fluff, eh," he spoke softly and, turning on his heels, he swept out of the room barking behind him, "Get 'em in order Trained Soldier. Hair cut, wash and shave, uniforms pressed, boots cleaned and after tea in bed by seven sharp ready for the morning. You're in the army now, my lads, and don't forget it."

"We're not ruddy likely to with you mate," whispered the lad at Rob's side and he could not help but snigger.

"Give those two a mark, Trained Soldier," Corporal Atkins poked his head around the door. He looked straight at the culprits. "Don't bother yourselves wondering lads. It's quite simple. I've got eyes in my arse and the back of my neck. I can see all, hear all and say just what I like. It's you bloody monkeys that have to say nothing. Give them the ablutions Trained Soldier."

He left and they relaxed and gathered to take instructions from the trained soldier. He softened somewhat when the corporal had left and patiently told them how to clean boots. "You gets the poker and sticks it in the old stove there and when it's red you burns the toecaps and spits on them with polish. You does it many times until you get them to look like this." He lifted the edge of his trousers and showed his glowing toecaps and shining boots.

Rob looked around the room for the stove and saw that the whole room was sparsely furnished with the bare necessities, but spotlessly clean. The floors round each bed were scrubbed until they almost gleamed. Each man was told that they were responsible for their own bed space and locker. That meant the area around their beds to the right and the locker that stood there to hold their belongings. Details were given out for certain duties, such as the washroom, the ablutions and the entrance. Rob had no idea what ablutions meant and found that they were the closets, and the corporal had ordered them to be cleaned out as a means of punishment.

They stood for hours pressing, polishing and cleaning. Nobody spoke a word until Trained Soldier stood and said, "That's it for now lads. Time for tea in the cookhouse." A bugle sounded and following Trained Soldier they ran outside and lined up. On the command "Right turn," chaos reigned. Some turned right, others turned left and some turned right round in a circle. Rob turned right and the man in front left and they clashed head on. Laughter rang across the square and Trained Soldier went purple with embarrassment.

"Right now lads, let's try it again. Which is your right, lad? And which is your left?" He went down the line and for almost an hour worked them through the routine until he was satisfied with the result. "Right turn," and to a man they turned. "By the left quick march." He had forgotten that one and found that nearly all had two left feet. In furious exasperation he took off his cap and threw it into the air screaming at the top of his voice, "Hold it there my lads. Right now, we'll begin again. On the order ..." And for another hour they went through the routine of left turn, right turn, left foot, right foot. "Right, let's give it another go. Altogether, right turn, by the left quick march." To a man they turned and marched in order, albeit in a jagged line, towards the cookhouse.

"You're not expecting cooked grub at this time of day are you? You've had that, we've only got bread and jam."

"That'll do," sighed Lobbs and they lined up to be handed two huge chunks of bread lathered with butter and jam and a mug of steaming hot strong tea that would have bent a spoon if there'd been sugar to stir into it. But Rob was so hungry he didn't give a hang.

"This all then, Trained Soldier?" one lad was foolish enough to ask.

"Yes, that's it. If you lot hadn't been so bloody slow and duff-footed we'd have had bacon and eggs and sausage and a bloody great lump of fried bread. But now, all of us, including me lad, has had this delicious meal of bread and jam. Next time we'll get it right shall we?" In chorus they shouted, "Yes Trained Soldier," and marched back to the block where again they cleaned, polished and pressed and finally fitted on their uniforms.

Rob looked in the mirror placed at the end of the room and preened himself. He turned this way and then that to get the full effect. He felt like a king.

"You needn't stand there lad. Get into your overalls. We've got to clean up now."

Rob and his laughing companion were given mops, buckets, cloths and scrubbing brushes. The buckets held chlorine and disinfectant and with it they scrubbed and cleaned the floors and bowls of the latrines. "You scrub everything, and I mean everything. You never know what lurks around these closets with some of the mucky buggers here."

Rob looked up at Trained Soldier. "VD lad. VD. You know what that is?" Rob nodded. He didn't really, but he'd heard it was a dreadful disease that turned you crazy and ate you all away.

As they scrubbed away, Rob began to hum and sing and soon the two young lads were singing some of the popular songs of the day. "Goodbye Dolly I must leave you...."

"You ain't in the army to enjoy yourself my lad. If scrubbing the latrines gives you that much pleasure, you can do it for the week."

Rob's chin tightened as he looked up to see Corporal Atkins standing above him, but he kept quiet and civilly said, "Yes Corporal."

Finally they had finished and went across to the cookhouse for a cup of cocoa and returned to the barrack room to fall into an exhausted, dreamless sleep.

He awoke to the shrill sound of reveille being blasted across the barrack square. Quickly he sprang out of bed and, gathering his things, went off into the washroom. A queue had formed and he waited, shivering and stripped to the waist until a basin was free. He washed and gave himself a good rub down with the towel and turned, intending to go back to the barrack room. A hand touched his shoulder. "Ain't you forgotten something lad?" Rob stared into Corporal Atkins' face. "You ain't shaved lad. In the army you shave every morning. Twice a day if you need it. But you don't, do you lad? You've still got a face like silk."

He stroked Rob's cheek with insolence and Rob had to exercise iron will not to pull away in disgust, but he looked fixedly into space. "Sorry Corporal. I forgot. I don't have to shave every day yet." He took out the mug, brush and soap and looked with fear at the blade of the cut throat razor. Fumbling, he lathered his face and held the razor to his chin. Twice he nicked his skin and blood poured into the white lather. Carefully he wiped his face and tried to stem the flow. "Dab it, lad, dab it." Rob used the caustic stick which stung his skin but stopped the flow of blood.

On returning to the barrack room he tidied up his bed space, folded his bed blankets into a neat pile and laid out his uniform as he had been shown. He and his mates waited with bated breath for the entry of Trained Soldier and Corporal Atkins.

The corporal strutted up and down and Rob had to admit that he was immaculate, smart and shining from head to toe. Casting his eyes over Rob's bed, the Corporal saw the clothes laid out correctly, the greatcoat rolled up tightly to knife width. "You had some training then lad? Ah yes, I recall, you spent a week here with Craddock. Not bad, lad, not bad for the first time. If you go on like this you'll get the stick. Know what that is lad?"

Rob answered smartly and with respect, "Yes Corporal." Maybe he wasn't such a bad bloke after all.

That first day went like lightning with physical training, drill, a visit to the rifle range, education, and weapon training. At nightfall they gathered again in the barrack room and began the work of cleaning, pressing and polishing.

"Do you know mate, I don't even know your name." The voice came from the man on the left.

Rob turned and looked at him. "I'm Clamp. Rob Clamp." He wiped his hand before holding it out in greeting.

"I'm Robson. Sonny Robson. We've been here nearly two days and none of us has hardly spoken a word."

Soon they were all greeting one another and telling some of their background. Each night they fell into bed and slept. Not a sound could be heard except deep breathing or relaxed, exhausted sleep.

After the first week Rob began to feel fit and strong and with a body and mind that reacted immediately to orders. His brain was alert and muscles showed where fat had once held limbs together. Every task brought something new to be learned, something to achieve. After the basic six weeks' training they were given a choice of regiment or trade. Rob had thought about it a lot and decided he would go for the Guards. Maybe he would get up to London and see the Queen. After all he was one of her soldiers.

During training he got the stick twice and for the first time he wished his mother could have known. They were all talking about going home on leave and he wondered what he would do. But he couldn't go back. His father would kill him.

"You've not been writing home, have you lad?" Trained Soldier asked one night. Rob shook his head. "You can't write then?" Rob nodded. "Well, write home then lad. You're doing well, they should be proud of you."

Rob decided to chance it and carefully wrote home, but did not put his address at the top of the letter. He simply said that he had joined up and was enjoying the life and was in the pink.

"If I was you lad, I'd get myself over to the Education Officer. You'll not get promotion without writing better than this," said Trained Soldier as he looked at the primitively addressed envelope.

Rob decided that that would be his next step. He could hardly believe the opportunities that lay before him. He was a soldier with money in his pocket and a chance to learn. What a life!

Basic training was almost over when disaster struck. One morning whilst on the rifle range Corporal Atkins came for him.

"Colonel wants to see you Private Clamp. In the office lad, at the double."

Together they ran across the square and arrived, puffing and panting, at the general office. Rob was petrified as thoughts raced through his mind. Were they going to chuck him out? But he could hear a familiar sound, his father's voice, coming from within the Colonel's office. He was the worse for drink and was shouting and bawling, "He's coming along with me, army or no bloody army. We've been looking for him high and low and it weren't until we got that letter we knew where to come. Postmark gave it away."

How daft could he get. Rob cursed himself as he listened to the tirade. The Colonel calmed his father down but he was adamant. Rob was to go home. He was under age and that was final.

Rob listened for a minute and then quickly turned on his heel and made to escape through the door. Corporal Atkins was too quick for him and grabbed him by the collar. "That ain't the way, lad. See what the Colonel can do. Say your piece and speak up. You ain't got anything to be ashamed of. The Colonel might be able to help." He looked at Rob's set face. "You're a good lad. Craddock was right. I thought he was gone a bit, sort of looked on you as the lad he never had, but he was right. You're a good soldier and we could do with more like you. Stick with it and say your piece."

The Colonel tried his best, but he didn't know father. "You can't make him go, Mr. Clamp. You can buy him out, but he has the right to stay if you can't pay up."

But Rob didn't know his father either because with a toss of the coin he paid the sovereign required for Rob's so called freedom. "He's coming home. Giving his mother all this trouble. I'll break his ruddy neck."

Rob stood silently as his father looked him over. "Well, I'll give you this, you've made a man of him you have. Never thought I'd live to see the day when this young devil would smarten up."

The Colonel tried to put in a good word, but his father would have none of it. "I don't want to go back sir, I don't want to work the chimneys. I want to be a soldier," Rob tried to speak up.

"You ain't going up bloody chimneys, lad. I got a better job than that. You're going to learn a good trade. I've got you in at Renshaw the blacksmiths. I'm teking you there tonight."

Rob couldn't believe his ears. His father had sold him in apprenticeship. That's where the money had come from. Feeling dull and empty he went to the stores and drew out his clothes. What a shabby bundle they made. He almost wept as he put on the short baggy trousers and ragged socks. He was surprised to find that he had grown taller and broader and the clothes were tight and uncomfortable. He looked such a pitiful sight and tried in vain to avoid Trained Soldier and Corporal Atkins as he left the barracks. But it was not be be and he hung his head in shame as he passed the squad marching to the cookhouse for dinner.

"Head up there, Private Clamp, march out smartly. Let's show 'em what we've taught you, lad. And don't be long afore you come back. We'll still be here," the Corporal shouted. Rob's head went up and, in step with his mates, he marched out of the big gates, not trying to hide the tears that now coursed down his cheeks.

CHAPTER 6

Rob walked head high until he heard the clang of the big gates close behind him. That was it. His army career was over before it had started. Thoughts raced through his mind in a jumble of cloud, and his shoulders drooped as realisation hit him. He looked a forlorn figure as he followed his father round the corner to the *Last Post* pub. He looked up at the name and sighed. "That's a laugh," he muttered.

"What you on about now boy?" his father asked and as Rob looked at the old man, his body crumpled from too many drinks over too many years, he wondered how on earth he managed to even stand. He was as near drunk as dammit, but was still walking and fully aware of what was going on.

They opened the swing doors of the pub and Tham, placing his hand on Rob's shoulder, pushed him forward. "Here he is then Master, as good and fine a lad as you'll ever see."

Renshaw lumbered towards the man and looked Rob up and down. "Aye, well, you found him then. He's not a bad looking lad. A bit of hard graft and we'll soon shape him up."

His words slurred into one another and Rob could see that to finalise the deal Renshaw and his father had been bevying for a good time. He was a man noted for his meanness and Rob thought that he looked a right old skinflint. His face was thin and narrow, topped with a good mop of wiry, greying hair that met a bushy beard at his ears. But he was strong and the leanness showed muscles that rippled under his threadbare jacket. He was also noted for his violent temper and stories were told of how many a young lad had felt the weight of his fist for not doing as he was told.

Rob decided to be like Atkins' three wise monkeys and just do as he was told and work towards getting back in the army as soon as he could. And at least he wouldn't have to bother about father.

"Fancy a drink then, boy?" Renshaw asked. At first Rob thought to refuse but he accepted a pint of stout.

Settling down in the corner of the wooden seat, Rob prepared himself for a long wait. They would have a drink or two before setting off and sitting there was as good as anything he would experience for a long time. He thought of Renshaw's place set at the bottom of the long lane at the back of Pipers Went Wood, a strange name and one that stuck in the mind. They passed him another drink and with a resigned sigh he took it and drank the lot almost in one go.

"Reckon you can hold your drink then do you youngster? Well, we'll see."

Rob couldn't make out whether Renshaw was being sarcastic or really trying to test his ability and by the third pint he neither knew nor cared. His head was swimming and his belly felt as if the whole regiment was doing drill around his navel. Tham and Renshaw were paralytic, but Rob could still make out what was going on around him. He felt muzzy, as if he was watching something from way above himself. "Have I died? Am I looking down on the silly sods from heaven?" But he knew he wasn't for he was thrown into a cart with such force that he rolled from one end to the other, and he was powerless to protest.

Someone belted the horse and away they went at a steady trot that twisted Rob's stomach with every turn of the wheel. His father and Renshaw lay at each side of him, belching with enough force to make a whirlwind. Suddenly Renshaw sat bolt upright as if struck by lightning and shouted at the horse, "Ger on, you lazy old bugger," and flayed the whip aimlessly above his head. The horse reared, and with a leap that would have cleared a barn roof, set off at the speed of light.

The cart rolled, swerved and swung about. His father rolled from top to bottom. Renshaw stood still, bolt upright at the front of the cart, eyes glazed and looking straight in front of him. The only trouble was that he was back to front and flaying the whip around Tham and Rob, missing them by inches as he whipped on his imaginary horse.

Rob clung to the edge of the cart and raising himself up tried to look over the edge. Frightened out of his life, he saw hedges and trees passing by in a rush of speed. How Renshaw kept standing, Rob couldn't make out. He must be like iron. His father would be black and blue, but it was every man for himself and with eyes tightly closed so that he couldn't see death coming, Rob prayed fervently to a God he had never even thought about before.

And then, just as suddenly, the old horse steadied up and peeping cautiously over the edge Rob saw that they had entered a cobbled yard where two or three men were gathered trying to steady the horse. Finally all was still. One man slung Renshaw over his shoulder and carried him into the house and Rob and Tham were slung into the stable alongside the horse. "You two can sober up in here," said a voice over his head, but Rob was past caring and with the sweet smell of hay in his nostrils he fell into a deep drunken sleep.

He was roused by a young lad shaking him by the shoulder and shouting in his ear, "Come on young 'un. Time to get up. Get yourself out there and swill down. My, you look a sorry sight." He laughed, but Rob was not amused. He sat up and looked around, scratching his back and removing wisps of straw from down his trousers. He looked for his father, but he had gone. Good riddance, too. The old bugger could be dead, for all he cared.

He followed the voice into the yard and stood rubbing his eyes to accustom them to the grey dawn light. Men were standing at the pump, stripped to the waist and swilling themselves down. Rob followed their example, taking off his jacket and shirt and leaning forward to let the cold water run over his face and body. The shock of the icy cold water hit his young body like a whiplash. Someone handed him a grubby piece of linen and he dried himself as best he could. The cloth was stiff and looked as if it hadn't been washed for a month. It smelled sour and as it hit his nose, he retched violently.

"Grub up," a coarse voice called from the door of the house. A woman was standing there, big boned and maybe handsome in her day. She wore a man's woollen shirt with the neck undone and sleeves rolled up to her elbows over a black skirt which reached down to her boots, also men's. A hessian apron covered the skirt, and the streaked marks of dried flour, matted food and polish showed where she wiped her hands as she worked.

Rob thought of the Ipswich barracks. The washhouses were luxury compared to this. Even the thought of Corporal Atkins brought a lump to his throat. His father had sold him for a few drinks. That was all he was worth as far as his father was concerned. But he would pay dearly for it for a very long time. Hatred set in his young heart and he vowed that one day he would get his own back.

He followed the men into the warm kitchen and sat down at the trestle table set near the door. The Master, as the men called Renshaw, sat at a proper table in the centre of the room. Rob looked down at the enamel plate on which lay a piece of blackened toast. In the middle floated a pool of grease. It looked like a stagnant lake in a burned out forest. Tea, or some sort of liquid, was poured into chipped enamel mugs. He couldn't take it and retched, rushing out into the yard before he threw up. He went to the pump and took in great gulps with such force that it took his breath.

Breakfast was over and the men filed back into the yard. "Come on, my lad. Get moving or you'll have the mistress after you."

Rob looked at the voice which belonged to a small, squat man of around forty. As he moved nearer, Rob could smell the unique scent of a horse having been shod. He sniffed. It filled his nostrils and brought about a thrill and a sense of belonging he had never known.

"I've been shoeing, lad, that's what you can smell. You've taken to it I see."

Rob tried to smile. "Well, I've always liked horses, but I never thought on being blacksmith."

"You'll be all right with me, lad. Charlie Abbot is the name. You're to be my lad." Rob's head inclined in question. "My lad. You're not ready to be apprenticed yet. Master likes to test you first, tries you for a month or so and then takes you on. He's a mean old devil, but it's the missus you want to look out for. She rules the roost and if you get on the wrong side of her you'll know about it."

Charlie walked across the yard and Rob followed. He went into the smithy and at first he could not see. Lights flashed across his eyes. It was dark and as his eyes cleared he could see rows and rows of irons lining the walls. Horse shoes of every size were hung on long nails. It looked like a cave.

"Here, try this for size." Charlie threw a length of blackened chamois leather across the anvil. Rob wrapped it around like an apron and tied it at the back. He was rewarded with a hammer hurtling through the air passed his ears. "Not like that, you silly young devil. Take it round and tie it in the front like this. If you bend and the horse catches you, you could have a nasty accident." Rob looked and copied.

"You work the bellows, nice and steady see, like this. You fetches and brings when I tell. Learn the size of the iron quick, boy. Master don't like time wasted in waiting."

Rob grasped the bellows and pumped them, at first too quick and then too slow, but after an hour or so he had the rhythm and was pumping steadily until a dull, red glow centred among the small black coal. He allowed himself to go into reverie. He watched fascinated as Charlie plunged lengths of iron into the fire until it was red hot, then he would plunge it into the butt of cold water at the side. It steamed and he would twist, bend and turn with the hammer until he got the shape he wanted. It was like an artist making pictures.

"Know what these are, boy?" Charlie asked.

Rob nodded. "Harrow teeth."

"Good lad. Them's going to be the best set you've ever seen when we've done and that's got to be afore tonight or the Master'll have my hide."

He swung round with a lump of iron and a flake of red hot ember fell on Rob's bare leg. Rob shouted and danced with pain.

"Heaven's boy, I'd not noticed you were still in shorts. What the hell they thinking on letting you in the forge like that? You'll be burned to death afore the morning's out." Charlie splashed the burn with water from the butt and frowned as he saw the patch of burnt flesh. "Go into the missus. Tell her what's happened and ask for some long pants, and don't be long."

Rob ran to the house as fast as he could with the pain searing into his shin. He knocked on the back door and stood waiting. He knocked again and a head appeared from the bedroom window.

"What you want then? You should be working hard, my lad, earn your keep." It was the missus.

Rob doffed his cap and stammered, "Please missus, I burnt my leg. I only got short trousers. Charlie Abbot said I was to come along to the house and get some long ones and my leg seen to."

"Let's look then." She leaned out of the window and Rob lifted his leg for inspection. "That ain't worth bothering with. I'm not coming all the way downstairs for that. Away with you and I'll look some pants out later. Get on. Time's money you know."

Rob dropped his foot on the floor and clattered back to the forge. His leg was now sore and as he bent his shin, the flesh pulled along the bone. He stopped by the pump and washed it down with cold water, wobbled and fell on his backside. A ripple of laughter almost as clear as the water came from behind.

"Here, I'll do that." A young woman grabbed the handle and began to pump. Rob stared at the vision of long fair hair tied back with a blue ribbon, a spotlessly clean white apron over a blue flowered dress that folded around dainty ankles above a pair of black side-buttoned boots.

"Where did you come from?" he asked and, remembering his manners, tried to doff his cap again. But it was all too much for his balance and he wobbled and fell again. The vision laughed and made to go forward to help.

"What the hell you about, boy ?" Renshaw stood above Rob and before he could move, a boot hit him in the backside with such force his head went forward and banged on the wooden casing of the pump.

"There's no need for that, Dad."

"You get back in the house. It ain't no place for you here," shouted Renshaw.

The girl ran and did as she was told and Rob struggled to his feet after putting on his sock and boot. His backside was sore and he rubbed it gently to ease the pain.

"That's my lass, young Clamp, and I know what your lot are like. You keep well away from her, right?"

Rob nodded. He wasn't interested in women anyway. He limped back to the forge and told Charlie what had happened. Charlie grunted and continued his work. Rob fetched and carried, caught his leg several times on the iron rods, bringing blood from the scratches. He was bruised from head to foot and his hands were blistered from pumping the fire. His backside ached and his heart was as heavy as lead.

"Tea's here." Rob carried on pumping as if in a trance. "Are you deaf, boy? Tea's here. Come on outside and tek a sup."

"Is it dinner time then?" Rob asked wearily and the men laughed.

"Good God no, boy. It's only eleven o'clock. No dinner until one."

Rob couldn't believe it. Only a few hours' work done and he was burned, bruised, cut and scratched and so fagged that he was fit to drop. Thankfully he sat down and took a mug of tea. It was sweet and strong and he drank it to the last drop, shaking the leaves out to dry at his feet. He leaned back and closed his eyes. Oh, to be back in Ipswich. Every bone in his body ached, and even without the kicking he was dead beat. That and the burns and cuts made it seem even worse.

"Move your arse, boy." But Rob didn't need to for another swift kick landed almost in the centre of his back and knocked him rolling across the cobbled yard. For a minute he lay, not believing what was happening. His first thought was to get up and retaliate, but he was far too tired, far too sore and far too sad to hit back. His spirit and his body were almost broken. "And I've only been here half a bloody day," he thought.

Charlie Abbot walked across to him and held out his hand as

Renshaw's voice bawled across the yard, "Leave the idle little bugger and I'll give him another punch up the backside to move him."

"I reckon you've done enough for one day, Master. Leave the boy be. I'll see to him," spoke Charlie quietly but with authority.

"Don't you tell me what to do on my own place or I'll..."

Charlie looked across at him. "You'll what, Master?"

"Oh, to hell with it," and Renshaw stalked off.

Charlie lifted Rob up and almost carried him to the forge. "Thanks mate," whispered Rob. "You shouldn't have done that. You could lose your job."

"Not much chance of that. And anyway, what if I did? A good smith can get a job anywhere and don't you forget that, lad. Don't let this lot put you off. Just get stuck in. Come on, rest on these bags at the side of the fire. I'll see to things." He saw Rob looking at him. "Don't you bother about Master. He won't come back here this afternoon."

And he didn't. Rob slept fitfully and then was roused to go into dinner. He crawled at the side of his new friend and slid into the bench at the kitchen table. Sheep's head broth and bread and butter pudding were set before them. In spite of his injuries, Rob ate heartily. The master was not in the house. "He'll have gone down to the tavern," whispered Charlie.

As they left the house to cross the yard, Rob felt a hand on his shoulder and turning saw Renshaw's daughter holding out something towards him. "It's some liniment for the burns and bruises. Here, take it quick afore Mother sees me."

Rob took the jar and stuffed it into his pocket. "What's her name?" he asked Charlie.

"Now don't you go getting any ideas about Missie Renshaw or you'll be in real trouble. The Master wants her for the hall. Make sure he gets all the work that way."

"I'm not interested in her for that. I just wondered what her name was, being she's so kind like."

"It's Mary, plain Mary Renshaw. Breaks all the hearts she does and as nice a girl as you could wish to meet. Don't know how the hell they managed it, but that's the truth," Charlie answered.

CHAPTER 7

The pay was a shilling a week, which Renshaw kept until the last Sunday in the month when each man was allowed a day off to visit his family. The married men who lived nearby in Hadleigh finished every Saturday night at five o'clock until Monday morning. At least they got away from the dreaded clutches of the Renshaws and were able to come back refreshed, if not enthusiastic, every Monday morning.

The lads and apprentices who lived in could go into Hadleigh on Saturday nights if they wished, but most of them were far too tired to do anything except hang around and play cards or just sleep enough to get the energy to face work again after the weekend. Sundays spent at Pipers Went entailed work; sweeping and swilling the yards, cleaning out the forge and seeing to the animals. There was no rest in the Renshaw's book for the wicked, or anyone else.

Throughout the first month, Rob worked steadily at each task given to him. After the first day's work, he went up to his stable room and found a pair of fustian grey trousers which, although not new, were in reasonable condition and they fitted fairly well except for the length of the leg. If he tightened his belt and strung them up, they didn't look too bad and they certainly protected his legs from injuries.

"Here you are then, boy, here's your brass. Get yourself a good wash and clean up and get off home early tomorrow. Show your old Dad what a good place you've got here." Renshaw threw the money down on the table in front of Rob who stared at him vacantly. "You've bin here four weeks, boy. It's your day off tomorrow. Don't you want the bloody money?"

But Rob was quick enough for that and he grabbed the money and stuffed it down his trouser pocket. He ate through the usual meal of fat bacon, mashed potatoes and cabbage, his brain ticking over rapidly. He had money, four shillings, and he had a day off. He couldn't wait to get out of this place.

Rob stood respectfully in front of the kitchen table where the family were eating their meal. To be fair, they ate the same as the men and Rob could not understand how Mary Renshaw could look as she did with the life they led. "Can I go tonight Master?"

Renshaw looked up and Rob saw streaks of greasy liquid fat rolling down his beard. The man was a beast and he was thankful at least that he didn't have to sit and watch him eat. God knows it was hard enough pushing the food down as it was, but to sit facing Renshaw would have taken Rob's appetite away completely. "What for?" asked Renshaw.

"Well, I've got a fair way to go, Master, further than the other lads and if I set off straight after work, not waiting for a meal, I'd get home tonight and have a good old day tomorrow. Doing both ways in one day wouldn't give me much time." The reason seemed to satisfy Renshaw and he nodded his assent.

Rob worked through the afternoon with a heart lighter than for many a week. He wasn't going home, no fear. Father would soon have the money from him. He was going into Stowmarket or some such place and spend his time there. He looked down at his trouser legs which dropped over his boot tops and ankles. They would have to be done before he walked the roads.

He hung around the pump until Miss Mary came out and then asked shyly, "Miss, have you such a thing as a needle and black thread I could borrow?"

She laughed at the strange request. "Whatever for?"

"I want to shorten my trousers. I can manage here with string to hold them up, but I don't want to go home looking like this. It wouldn't do your Dad's image any good, would it?"

"I'll bring it up later on."

Rob knew he was asking her to do something that would cause a great deal of trouble if she was found out. But, he reasoned, she didn't have to do it if she didn't want to. It was up to her.

Mary waited until the coast was clear and everyone had gone from the yard and then climbed the ladder stairs and handed a needle and thread to Rob through the narrow doorway. "Can you see then?" she asked. Rob shrugged his shoulders and struggled to thread the needle. "Oh come here boy, let me do it." He looked up at her, his head to one side, and smiled. "Toss them down the ladder and I'll sit and do them. I can see where they want to go from the crease where you've turned them up."

He waited and listened until he heard her feet touch the concrete floor at the bottom of the steps and then downed his pants and threw them down. He peeped around the door and watched as she stitched away, biting the thread with her teeth as she finished her task.

"There you are." She threw them up at him. It was a great job and they fitted a treat. He smiled his thanks and when she asked what he was going to do for the day he just said, "Don't really know," and left it at that. He wasn't sure why he didn't want to lie to Miss Mary but felt it was better to say nothing rather than embark on some wild story.

About seven o'clock that night he set off, boots shining and as clean as a new pin after scrubbing himself so well under the pump that Charlie had asked him if he was going to leave any skin on his back. "Just wanted to get this place out of me, that's all," he told him.

"You not happy then, boy?"

Rob rubbed himself vigorously with the ragged cloth and muttered, "I hate the bloody place," with such vehemence it took Charlie aback.

"Well, make sure you come back, and on time, or the Master'll hunt you down like a rabid fox."

When he finally got away he felt good to be on the road, and after a while began to sing to himself. Soon he drifted into the army songs and he found himself marching in step to them, arms swinging, shoulder high. But, as realisation dawned on him, he slumped again and felt the helplessness of his position. He thought of running away, but where could he go? He couldn't go to the Craddocks, that would only cause bother. It was better to stick it out as Atkins had said, and legally get out as soon as he could.

The next problem was what to do with himself. He had enough money for a night's lodging, but how would he pass the time? He stopped at the first pub and ordered a pint of mild and bitter. Downing it with such speed, the landlord stared in amazement. "My word, boy, you needed that," he said.

Rob ordered another and downed that more slowly. He began to feel good, his aches, pains and hurts disappearing as he drifted into oblivion. He loved the work but hated the place and the Master. The only good things were Charlie Abbot and Miss Mary. He ordered another drink to drown his sorrow and soon felt as if the beer was swilling around like a high tide. He did remember being thrown out of the pub at closing time and landing in the gutter, but then blessed oblivion took over and he knew nothing more until he woke between clean sheets in a little iron bed.

As he lifted his head to look around the room, it throbbed and felt like lead. He could just recognise another bed on the opposite wall and whispering asked, "Where the hell am I?"

"You're in the army."

Rob sat bolt upright. "In the what?"

"The army," answered the voice.

"What barracks?" Rob was trembling. They would never believe that he hadn't intended to run away.

"Barracks be buggered. You're in the Salvation Army. They picked you up on the meat run last night and brought you here."

Rob sank back on his pillow with a sigh of relief and then remorse. What a thing to come to. He felt lonely, frightened and, most of all, ashamed. Maybe he should have gone home after all. They said no good would come if you lied. Well, that had been proved to him many a time. Would he never learn? "What's the time?" he asked.

"How the hell do I know. I ain't a ruddy king. I don't own a watch."

Rob didn't bother to wait any longer and, grabbing his clothes together, he galloped down the stairs and out into the street. He stood on the pavement and thought. Best get back, he decided and set off, almost running every step of the way to Pipers Went. He didn't want to go back, but if he stayed he might just get himself into more trouble and that would go against him when he was ready to join up. Anyway, it was better to get back and get the actual pain of arriving over with.

As he entered the yard somewhat breathless, Miss Mary spotted him and, waving greetings, came to meet him. "Had a good time, Rob?" she asked.

He just nodded and ran up to his bed, lying down and falling asleep immediately without even taking his clothes off.

That week he simply worked and slept, closing his heart and mind to all that went on around him. He did exactly as he was told, taking great care not to get into any trouble. The only highlights were the few snatched moments spent with Miss Mary.

"You're going to make a good blacky, Rob. Come on, get a hold on that hammer and have a go with me." Charlie looked to encourage good lads that shaped up and Rob was one of the best he had ever had in this place. He watched as the lad stood in front of the anvil and hammered with the rhythm that only a born blacksmith can get.

The hours passed slowly, but on the Sunday, instead of spending the extra allowed half hour in bed, he got up and decided to miss breakfast and take a walk down the lane across the fields. He hit the half way mark and decided to turn round so as not to be too late, when Miss Mary appeared, walking to meet him. She must have seen him set off. Surprisingly the thought did not please him. At that moment he really wanted his own company, but as they got talking he softened and began to tell her of his ambitions to join the army and to be a farrier. She told of her father's ambitious marriage plans for her. She would much rather have been a teacher and have the freedom to find her own husband.

"What sort of bloke are you looking for then?" he asked with innocence.

"Well, wouldn't mind one like you," she whispered, grabbing his hand and giving it a gentle squeeze.

Rob was too taken aback to respond and she darted off in the opposite direction calling out, "Best be off now. Wouldn't do for father to catch us. He'd kill you."

But he felt good. And why should Renshaw want to kill him? He wasn't a bad specimen of manhood, well lad-hood. Then commonsense prevailed and he knew just why he was not a good prospect for Miss Mary Renshaw. He had nothing, he was nothing and at the rate he was going he would never be anything. But one day, one day, he would show them.

The positive thoughts cheered him up and he whistled all the way back to the yard and spent the rest of the day doing his chores with a much lighter heart. It was nice to feel wanted, even if it was a pipe dream.

When he got back to the yard one of the other lads announced he had a visitor. Rob knew it could only be his father and wondered what he wanted.

"Come to fetch you for the day, my boy. Got the cart and old Nellie. Your Mother's been worried about you and it'll do her heart good to see you."

Rob knew the old man well. He knew it had nothing to do with his mother's wishes. He wanted Rob's wages. Rob began to laugh and then couldn't stop. It got out of control. His belly shook and tears rolled down his cheeks. Tham stared in amazement as Rob said, "You're too bloody late, you silly old bugger. You ought to learn to count, father. I had my day off last week, and I spent my wages. I ain't due any more for three weeks." And without looking back he ran up the ladder and threw himself on the bed, still shaking with laughter. It wasn't often he got one over his father and the thought of it did him a power of good.

Tham stood bewildered in the yard for a few minutes and then got into the cart. Flaying the horse in anger, he left muttering wild oats against his son.

Rob completed his Sunday chores and then slept. After tea he decided on another walk, maybe going down to the village to call on Charlie Abbot and his missus. He knew he would be welcome.

The village of Wattisham was small, consisting only of a green surrounded by thatched cottages, a school and a church. Rob sat down on the bench outside the pub for a while without a thought of a drink. Anyway, he didn't have a brass farthing on him but he was content to breathe in the soft air and have nothing to do but stare into space and dream.

Walking back in the dusky mist of the country evening he heard familiar footsteps following and without turning round knew that it was Miss Mary. "Where you been then?" he asked.

"To visit my aunt in the village. I saw you on the bench and thought we might walk together. It's nice to have company this time of evening."

It was a good story, but Rob knew she had been watching his every movement. Shyly, he took her hand and they walked, chatting away about their young hopes and dreams. He told her that one day he wanted a thatched cottage to own and his own smith. That was after a spectacular army career of course. "Might have a few pigs and chickens and that," he said.

"And a wife?" she asked.

Rob hunched his shoulders and, looking at her, winked cheekily. They stopped at the small gate that led into Pipers Meadow and he placed his arm, with great daring, around her shoulders. She moved closer and they sat without saying a word, content and happy in each other's company.

"What the bloody hell's this then?"

Rob jumped, and turning round saw it was the mistress in full flight, running across the meadow towards them. He jumped down from the gate and caught his jacket on the hook, tearing the seam from top to bottom. It unbalanced him and he lay stunned as the massive heap of black and sacking came towards him brandishing a hay fork in her hand.

Rob almost laughed at the thought of how she looked like Boadicea on the back of a penny. But it was no laughing matter. She moved swiftly and made to stick the prongs in his backside. In spite of his quick movements one caught his buttock in the flesh and he yelped with pain.

"You daft old bugger. You're barmy. What harm were we doing?" Rob shouted back, between howls of pain.

"Enough harm to pack your bags. Go on. You're sacked," she shouted, making another plunge.

Rob didn't need telling twice and, without looking at the sobbing idol of his dreams, took to his heels and ran as fast as he could, blood streaming down his legs and into his boots.

What was he to do now? He had no job and no money, his backside was hanging out of his trousers, blood was filling his boots and pain was wracking his legs. Atkins words "You can always come back, lad," rang through his mind. That's it. He would go back to Ipswich and join up. They couldn't stop him now. With his mind made up, he walked quickly, the pain almost forgotten in his eagerness to reach his friends again.

His courage almost failed him at the thought of the long miles ahead, and when the rolling wheels of a cart stopped he looked expectantly at the driver who asked if he could help.

"If you please, sir, I've had a bit of an accident on the farm gate and hurt my, er, buttock. I need to get to Ipswich."

"Well, jump in lad. I'll take you to the outskirts. I'm going to Swaffam, but it wouldn't hurt to help a wounded soldier!"

For a while they drove in silent harmony, the man taking sideways looks at his passenger. And then they began to talk. Rob said he was learning, or rather had been learning, the blacksmith's trade.

"Where are you going to now?"

Rob told the man he was going to visit some friends who would look after him for a while.

They finally stopped on the outskirts of Ipswich and the man got down to help Rob from the cart. He held out a white card. "Look, I think you might be in some kind of trouble, but I know you are a good lad and it isn't your fault, so take this card and keep it safe. If you ever need help, contact me. You promise that?"

Rob nodded and stared at the vanishing cart after reading the card with the words "Major P.M. Withers, Royal Horse Guards,

Wellington Barracks, London" printed on it.

Just as dawn broke he stood hammering on the door of the Craddocks' house. They would just be getting up. "What's all this then. Well, just come and look here mother." The sergeant drew him inside and Mrs. Craddock jumped up in pleasure to greet him. "What's been going on. Are you in some trouble?" The sergeant looked at the bloodstained trousers and the soaking boots and turned him round. Rob told his sorry tale.

"Well, you are a ragged arsed militia boy and no mistake. Come on, deary, let's get you all cleaned up."

"You say a woman did this?" The sergeant started to laugh. "I wouldn't tell old Atkins or he'll never let you live it down." But he wasn't really amused and after they had cleaned Rob up and dressed what was really a small wound they sat and watched as he ate his breakfast.

"What are you going to do with him, sergeant?" Mrs. Craddock asked.

"What do you want to do, boy. It's up to you?"

"I want to join up again and proper this time and learn my trade as a blacky." He spoke between mouthfuls of food.

"Then that's what you'll do."

Rob felt confident as the sergeant spoke and thankfully accepted the old nightshirt and went off to get some sleep.

Sergeant Craddock brought Corporal Atkins home for dinner and he tut-tutted throughout the whole story. "And you reckon on the army then?" he asked Rob, who nodded fiercely.

Rob spent the rest of the day sleeping and helping Mrs. Craddock who treated him rather like an invalid, which he rather enjoyed.

"You're coming up to the barracks in the morning, lad. Best get him smartened up, mother, but don't mend the trousers or anything. Just see he's clean."

As they approached the barracks, the man and the lad marched together through the double gates. Rob remembered how he had walked out and his head went up in defiance. He looked at the familiar yard and then stopped as his eyes became fixed on a familiar object — his father with the horse and cart at the ready.

"Steady boy, steady. You just stand there," whispered Sergeant Craddock.

His father disappeared with the Sergeant and Corporal Atkins into the Colonel's office and after a few minutes they called Rob in.

He stood to attention and faced the Colonel. His father looked rather pleased with himself, but Rob's heart sank.

"I understand you want to take up an army career again, Clamp, following the right channels this time," the Colonel addressed Rob.

"Yes, sir," he answered smartly.

"Have you brought the references?" He was now addressing old Tham who proffered several pieces of paper.

"Yes, sir. One from the chemist, the doctor, the schoolmaster and the parson. There are seventeen altogether."

"Two would have done, Mr. Clamp. But never mind. And here's your bounty. Ten guineas I believe. You sign here to give up all rights to the boy."

Rob turned to look at the sergeant and the corporal who stood stoney faced to attention. Sergeant Craddock winked.

"You sign here, Clamp." The Colonel pushed a piece of paper towards Rob who quickly did as he was told. "Right. You're in the army now, lad, really in the army. Congratulations."

Rob shook the offered hand and turning, could not stop himself from hugging his heroes, Craddock and Atkins.

"Steady on there, Private Clamp," laughed Corporal Atkins and they took an arm each and carried him outside.

"Where did the money come from?" Rob asked.

"Well, me and the Corporal here put together and the Colonel made it up out of the funds. And now we've got you, all bought and paid for."

Rob felt as if his heart would burst with joy and as his father left he even managed a wave and a cry of, "Safe journey." He couldn't believe that they had done all this for him.

"It ain't just for you, boy. It's for the army as well. And don't you forget, I want my money's worth."

"And so do I," laughed Atkins and ruffled Rob's hair.

Rob sprang to attention and saluted smartly. "I'll see to that gentlemen. I'll do my best. I'm well ready."

"What for?" the sergeant asked.

"To be a real soldier," and he emphasised the word with a ring of confident authority.

"And I bet you'll do us proud," laughed Corporal Atkins as the trio marched across the barrack square.

CHAPTER 8

Rob's return to the army was a major turning point in his life. He had cut the ties with home and although Sergeant Craddock and his wife told him there was always a welcome at their place, he was now totally independent. There was only himself to rely on. He was now his own man.

The thought did not deter him at all and all through his basic training it was obvious that this young soldier had only one ambition — to be the best. Had it not been for his reading and writing, he would have been the best recruit of that intake. His education let him down slightly on the final points, but he came a very close second.

Having had a short taste of the life, he knew what to expect and was prepared. The Colonel had insisted that he be placed in a different squad from Corporal Atkins, but he and Sergeant Craddock kept "their beady eye" on his progress and he came up to all expectations. In drill there was no other recruit to touch him. He reacted to discipline with an inborn instinct that surprised even his two benefactors, and to see him strutting across the parade ground warmed the cockles of the drill sergeant's heart.

The lack of reading and writing did not worry him. He had no intention of a job behind a desk or in the stores and right from the start he had made it clear that he wanted to be a farrier.

The Trained Soldier warned that he would have to be good to get put to a trade, but Rob was a natural. If given authority he carried out the orders with controlled efficiency, providing everything went according to plan. If there was any messing around, he could throw a quick, violent temper that startled with its viciousness. And, surprisingly, he showed no remorse whatever.

The first time this side of his nature came to light was during the nightly bulling session. Rob took pride in the way his boots gleamed and would hold them up to the window or the light to catch the reflection. His uniform was pressed to perfection and his webbing was ivory white.

The Corporal in Charge was Arnold Sharp, a good soldier with a pleasant attitude that got the best out of the lads. He knew when to encourage, when to blast them, and when to sympathise. Rob liked him and reacted to his quiet authority with respect.

His favourite saying was, "Wait for it lad, wait for it. Play your cards right, and, let it go." The young lads applied this to many situations, a favourite one being in the barrack room as they lay on their beds, bellies full of stodgy food and wind!

Towards the end of the course, one of the lads managed to get some beer smuggled into the block. Rob told them in no uncertain terms that they were "Bloody fools. If you're caught, you'll get chucked out," he warned, but young and foolhardy as they were they took not one bit of notice. Rob would not have any part of it and lay on his bed dozing until lights out was sounded. His reverie was broken by the lads jumping over the beds, rolling underneath them and finally chucking the pillows across the room.

"You daft devils. Corporal Sharp'll be here in a minute and if he sees this lot we'll be for it," shouted Rob. Their reply was to taunt him because he would not join in.

"Here, come on, let's make the miserable old bugger have a sup," shouted Jimmy Rack, and jumping on top of Rob he tried to force drink down his throat and in doing so spilled the foaming beer down his shirt. In a frighteningly vicious attack, Rob shot up and landed a right hook with such force that it sent Rack sprawling across the next bed with blood spurting from his mouth and nose.

"Now," panted Rob, "Get this bloody mess cleaned up. We'll be on jankers for a fortnight if Sharp sees this."

His main thought was a fear of being back squadded. Rob had no intention of going through training a third time. He got up, wiped the mess from his shirt and shouted orders to rouse those who were the worse for wear. Rack had collapsed in a heap and as Rob stepped over him, his whole body heaved.

"Wait for it lad, wait for it. Play your cards right," Rob shouted and bending down flung Rack over his shoulder and ran like hell to the latrines. Rack retched with every step, but nothing came up. Rob dumped him on the cold stone floor and, filling the enamel jug with icy water, proceeded to sprinkle his face.

"Chuck the lot over himn," a voice said impatiently.

"What's the good on that. He'd be wet through and spew all over the place. He'll be round in a minute. You get back and see that all's tidy." Rob was still angry but was now in control of the situation and having seen the power of his fists, the others obeyed his orders without question. As Rack sobered up, Rob carried him back to the block.

"Stand by your beds," Corporal Sharp's voice rang through the corridor.

"Stand up you silly bugger," Rob whispered and as if by a miracle, Rack sprang to attention.

Corporal Sharp walked slowly up and down the room. He sniffed the air but said nothing, except to tell Rack to get himself cleaned up. "You'd best go sick tomorrow if you're no better. You look quite peaky, lad. Anyone been drinking here, Clamp?" he asked quietly.

"Not as I know of, Corporal," Rob answered, eyes to the front and voice firm.

The Corporal walked on and then, turning at the door and with a face as straight as a poker, said, "You get caught short in the night, Clamp?" Rob stared and Corporal Sharp pointed with his stick to a row of bottles placed neatly underneath his bed. "I know it's a long way to the urinals, but that's going it a bit lad." Rob smothered a smile. "And if you have another shin-dig, remember the old corporal likes a drop now and again."

His status went sky high with every man in that room, and with military precision they sprang to attention and, smiling, loudly answered, "Yes Corporal."

After that Rob was treated with respect. Nobody asked about Rack's mouth and nobody mentioned the incident again.

On the day of the passing out parade, Rob prepared his uniform carefully. The lads had been told that they could invite their parents if they wished, but Rob didn't want that. They wouldn't have come and anyway his mother had nothing decent to wear. If his father came, it would be for the free booze, not for any pride in his son. He knew Sergeant and Mrs. Craddock would be there, and he would do his best to make them proud of him.

They assembled on the parade square and as the order was given and the band struck up, Rob's whole body tingled. He marched left marker, head held high and with a pride that showed in every step. The Lord Lieutenant of Suffolk took the salute and as Rob turned his head to the right he saw, out of the corner of his eye, his sister Mary, done up as pretty as you please and looking as proud as Punch.

After dismissal he walked across to her and pulled back as she made to embrace him. "Mind my uniform gel. How did you get here then," he said in one rushed breath.

"Your friend, Sergeant Craddock, wrote care of the vicar and he gave the letter to me. Oh, don't fret yourself, Father won't come. He brought me right enough, but I gave him five shillings and left him in the pub." She took Rob's arm and they walked over to the refreshment marquee.

"And who's the girlfriend, Clamp?" asked Corporal Sharp.

Rob introduced them and after a few minutes he was forgotten. His sister Mary and Corporal Sharp had only eyes for each other and Rob let them get on with it, only seeing Mary again to say goodbye.

"Where are you off to now then?" she asked. "We must keep in touch."

"I'm off to Aldershot. I got a posting there as apprentice farrier."

"Well, I must say you've turned out better than I ever dreamed you would."

"That's the army for you miss. Makes a man out of a boy," said Corporal Sharp.

"Yes, I can see that," Mary laughed, holding on to his arm as if she was about to drop in a dead faint if she let go.

Rob had passed with flying colours in all the practical areas, and little attention was paid to his academic work. Being a blacksmith meant strength of mind and body and he had plenty of that. There was no need for writing on a horse's foot.

He left Ipswich with some sadness. Mrs. Craddock cried and even the Sergeant showed some emotion as they shook hands. "Now, remember where we are. Keep in touch, and you're welcome any time. Be a good lad and work hard. I'm proud of my little ragged arsed lad," she said.

But Rob was keen to get on with his career and settled into Aldershot very quickly to begin his army life in earnest.

The Farrier Corporal in Charge was George Sutton, a man from the north and he saw from the first day that Rob intended to work hard and make the army his life. Knowing a little about smithing gave Rob an advantage over the other lads and he was soon given some responsibilities. Reveille was at 5.30 am and after swilling down and dressing, they fed the horses. After that they had breakfast before mustering on the parade ground and being detailed to work.

"How long will it take afore I'm finished my time?" Rob asked.

"You lad, about three years I should think afore you're a journeyman," answered Corporal Sutton.

That time was set in Rob's mind and he worked with a determined will until finally, at the age of eighteen, he was passed as a blacksmith journeyman. The next thing was a posting, and he waited eagerly to see which regiment he would get and where he would go.

"Where would you like to go, Private Clamp?" the Movements Officer asked.

"Well, I've always fancied London, sir, to see the Queen and all that."

"See the sights eh? You got a lady friend then, Private?"

Rob shook his head. In all the time he had been at Aldershot, he had never once taken a girl out. Oh, he had laughed and joked with them when he went out with the lads for a night out. He had even kissed one or two girls in fun, but all his energy had been given to the army. His leaves had been spent with the Craddocks and he had no wish to encumber his life with a woman as yet. Manoeuvres and working hard to make horse shoes by the hundred to send out to the Boer War had kept his mind and body fully occupied.

When his posting finally came, he couldn't believe his luck. He was going to London to the Household Cavalry division to be a real soldier of the Queen. He packed his kit, collected his rail warrant and caught the early train. As he travelled he thought of the shabby lad who had walked all those miles to join the army. He eased his uniform as he sat down. Creased and pressed to knife edge standard, buttons shining and hat to one side, his reflection showed in the window a tall young man, not handsome, but with an odd, attractive air about his being. He smiled and settled down in the red plush seats for the journey in comfort and ease.

He fingered the chevron that showed he was a farrier and, closing his eyes, listened to the rhythm of the wheels: I'm going to London to see the Queen, and London's somewhere I've never been. The words went over and over in his mind. London, the heartbeat of the world. What more could he wish for?

CHAPTER 9

"Just break the news to mother," Rob's tuneless voice joined in the well-known chorus being thumped out on the pub piano by one of his new mates, Sonny Hall. Mixed voices rang through the bar with drunken emotion at the climax of the song which told of a poignant message left for his mother by a soldier dying on the battlefield.

Rob loved every minute of this. The whole of his life was good: he loved his work in the palace, living in the barracks and, most of all, being in the centre of London. Everything about the life fascinated and thrilled him. The fashions of both the men and the women were something he had never even dreamed of. How on earth did they get into those tiny wasp-waisted dresses? How did the blokes keep those curled moustaches in place so perfectly? He was given permission to grow a moustache and, after instructions from the barber, sported quite an excellent one with pride.

He had grown tall and at nineteen was still lean, but with a strength of character that made him popular amongst his comrades. His two new friends were Sonny Hall and Walter Barnes, two other young farriers who made up a trio of right young devils who were the bane of many a young maiden's heart.

As part of his training, Rob was taught to ride and one of his biggest thrills was the mounted parades from the barracks to the palace. He lapped up the adulation of the crowds and, most of all, the way the girls vied for his attention.

"It's the uniform that gets them, boy, and we sure are fine looking specimens of manhood," laughed Walter as they inspected each other before going out on the town. Walt, Rob and Sonny were spruced up in their best blues with red stripes down blue trouser sides, short red jackets with shining brass buttons and pillbox hats cheekily perched on their heads with chin straps resting beneath lower lips. They had their pay in their pockets and were ready for the world.

"It's no good going to this place," Sonny said as they approached the usual *Shamrock* pub. "Get's a bit crowded on Fridays. Let's go up town."

"Splendid idea old boy, don't you know. Let's take a carriage and hit the high life," Rob mocked, in a perfect take-off of an officer.

Instead of a carriage they boarded an open topped tram and travelled through the streets, whistling after the young girls and saluting the older generation. This really was the life for Rob and, for a second, his mind flew back to home. What a far cry this was from the rundown cottage and ragged clothes. The only contact he kept was by sending the odd shilling or two to his sister through the vicar in the hope that she would pass it onto his mother. He never enclosed an address and could only hope that his father didn't get his hands on it.

"Where to now, gentlemen?" he asked as they got off the bus in the centre of the bustling city.

"To the Palladium, the London Palladium, where else boy?" Walt answered, and they strutted down the streets through a small park surrounded by tall white houses and finally to the Palladium where a crowd thronged through the open doors of the theatre.

Rob had often heard of this famous place where Vesta Tilly and the famous Jersey Lily performed. He was rather put off by the small back street and the narrow doorway, but once in the entrance foyer he stood in amazement at the splendour of the red, blue and golden colours on the walls and ceiling. Plants so high they were like trees stood at the foot of the stairs which had a golden bar for the ladies to hold whilst they lifted their skirts discreetly to go into the boxes and balcony. The Ipswich theatre had been nothing like this. He waited whilst Sonny got the tickets and stared in fascination at the scene. The men wore bow tie and tails and ladies were dressed in flowing silk and satin of all colours that fell in folds from bare creamy shoulders. It was like a dream.

"Programme, sir?" a voice from the left spoke softly. Turning round, Rob was confronted by a very smart young lady in an outfit of royal blue corded silk covered by a white lace trimmed apron and peeping from below her skirt he saw a pair of tiny feet enclosed in soft black pearl-buttoned boots. Her hair, neatly coiled, was tied back with a matching blue bow. Rob had never seen servants like this, even at the manor. But she wasn't a servant, she was an usherette or programme seller, one of many in red or blue costumes. Small lads, aged no more than eleven or twelve, were rushing about all over the place almost exact replicas of soldiers with their pillbox hats and brass buttons. The commissionaire in top hat and tails had a resplendent military bearing and gave the finishing touch to the plush atmosphere.

"Come on mate, get a move on or we'll not get a good seat." Walt nudged his arm and propelled him towards the auditorium which held a feeling of exciting anticipation. A hush fell as the curtains fell back on a row of colourful dancing chorus girls. The show consisted of a juggler, comedian, singer and magician. The star attraction and last act was Marcardo the Great Reader of the Mind, and as he took the stage the audience waited for his act to begin. He was assisted by a dark-skinned young lady of eastern origin dressed in flowing purple robes and adorned with a profusion of gold jewellery. The act was truly amazing and the audience applauded loudly.

"Now, ladies and gentlemen, to end this presentation we shall need two volunteers, two brave young people of the male gender to come up on stage and help me out. Come on gentlemen, you won't be sorry, I promise you that," Marcardo called down in to the audience and, shading his eyes, pretended to look deep into the darkened rows. Two chorus girls appeared, scantily dressed in costumes of pink feathers and satin, and danced along the stage and into the audience. As they passed Rob their perfume filled the air making him feel quite heady. They turned and spotting the three heroes called to them saying, "Come on soldier, you look a likely candidate."

The girl took Rob's arm and he willingly followed her down to the stage. Walter was dragged, playfully protesting, after him and Sonny was left behind grumbling, "Those two have all the luck." It was all good innocent fun, and Rob joined in with enthusiasm.

"Oh, very nice, soldiers of the Queen. I always thought that you were told never to volunteer lads. But come on here, you're more than welcome. Two smart lads like you would liven up any act." Rob's heart swelled with pride as Marcardo prattled on with his patter. "Sit down on these nice comfy chairs and take it easy, take the weight off your feet." They sat down in two plush chairs and made to settle themselves into their cosy depths. "Now lean back and close your eyes. No peeping, you naughty boy." Marcardo tapped Rob's hand, making the audience laugh. They lay back and Marcardo started his mind reading act. "You are a blank. Well, that's what the army does for you. And as for you," he was now addressing Rob, "All I can say is good luck lad, you'll need it!"

The audience roared and Marcardo continued his performance by calling for silence. "This is the serious bit, lads. Now sit absolutely still and concentrate."

The perfume filled Rob's nostrils and he realised that the young lady was sitting on his knees. Before he could open his eyes, she placed her hand around the back of his neck and pressed her lips down on his mouth. At first he struggled, trying to open his eyes and see what was going on, and then he pretended to give in and kissed her with such passion that she struggled to free herself.

"Oh my word, I don't think I could repeat what's in your mind at this moment," said Marcardo, and the audience roared with laughter. He then turned to Walt. "Now keep your eyes shut soldier. It's your turn now."

The feathered costume settled on his knee and Walt made the most of it, kissing her passionately until an angry voice interrupted, "Here, get out of it, that's my missus, that is." A stooge from the audience chased Walt back to his seat and the laughter filled the air till it echoed and bounced back from the walls.

"Thanks for being such sports, lads. Here, take these two complimentary tickets," said Marcardo.

"There's three of us, sir. We go everywhere together," Rob replied.

"What, everywhere?" and Marcardo sportingly gave Rob three tickets as he returned to his seat amid applause.

After the show the three decided to visit the pub just around the corner and as they entered the smoky, dim lit saloon they soon realised it was a show business pub. Rob listened to the snippets of conversation with great interest as he waited for the drinks to come. He was well ready for a pint and lifted the glass to his lips with a deep breath ready to drink when the familiar perfume filled the air around him and he put his drink down without taking a drop. The chorus girl was sitting at the next table and even in the dim light he could see her beauty. Fair hair curled around her creamy skinned face and hazel eyes. Her coat was grey velvet with a fur collar which framed her neck and chin and highlighted her colouring. He couldn't take his eyes off her and watched as she lit a cigarette and placed it in a long tortoiseshell holder.

Walt nudged his elbow. "We'll be kicked out if you gawp like that." He laughed, but it was no good. Rob was completely fascinated.

Taking his courage in both hands, Rob walked over to the girl and in a polite, distant voice that sounded as it if was coming from the other side of the room, asked, "Can I buy you a drink, miss? I ain't being forward like. I'm the soldier from the theatre, the one on the stage."

She appeared not to have noticed and continued talking to her companions. Rob made to move away, feeling daft, and then her head moved and her eyes travelled from his boots all the way up his uniform to meet his gaze. They stared into each other's face and she smiled a dazzlingly white smile. "OK, soldier. A large gin please."

Rob went into action and brought her drink, taking care to place it down at her side. She patted the seat at her side and he sat down.

"Got a name then?"

"Er, yes, miss. Clamp, miss. Rob Clamp, farrier with the Household Cavalry."

"Is that so. Well, I'm pleased to meet you. I'm Amelia." She held out her hand and Rob felt the velvet texture of her skin. He was entranced and no amount of persuasion would move him from her side to return to the barracks with his mates.

"Well, we're off mate. See you get back on time. All right?"

Rob nodded, now under the influence of several pints. "Don't worry. I'll be all right," he slurred.

Sonny and Walt hovered around for a while and then, with a shrug, left him to his own devices.

How many drinks he had he neither knew nor cared and he soon lost count of the number of gins downed by his beloved Amelia. He recalled wanting to take her home and being refused and he vaguely remembered being thrown out of the pub, piled into a cab, dragged out and thrown on to his bed. Oblivion took over until his deep dreamless sleep was rudely awakened by reveille, sounding as if all the bells in hell had been let loose.

"Good God, what happened?" He sat up and held his throbbing head in his hands. "How did I get back here? Did she ..."

"No, she bloody didn't. We brought you back. We waited for you. That floosie wouldn't have given a damn if you got back or not. Her sort is only interested in what they can get out of a bloke," Walter snapped with unusual venom. "Get a move on or you'll be on a charge."

His two mates pulled him off the bed and he staggered to the washhouse rinsing his head several times with cold water to ease the thudding pain. Back in the block he found his kit laid out and his uniform ready for parade.

"Don't just stand there, get dressed you silly bugger," and with urging from both Sonny and Walt, Rob got dressed just in time for the orderly officer's parade.

They assembled and Rob stared straight ahead as the officer walked up and down the ranks. He stopped, facing Rob and called out, "Fall out Lance Corporal Clamp." Rob was not paying attention and certainly didn't expect to hear his name. "Fall our Lance Corporal Clamp. Don't you know your bloody name?" Rob jumped forward smartly. "Congratulations Clamp. You deserve a promotion."

The salute was returned and, stepping back in line, Rob whispered to Sonny, "Did you know about this?"

"Not until we read orders this morning. Why do you think we took all that trouble?" Walt slapped Rob on the shoulder as they went to the cookhouse.

"Watch it lad, or I'll pull rank?" joked Rob.

"That'll cost you a drink or two tonight and no mistake."

"Not tonight mates, I've got to see somebody."

"Not that floosie. You don't want to get mixed up with them showgirls, Rob. They're not for the likes of us mate," Sonny gave a serious warning.

"Who said anything about showgirls? And don't you fret about me. I can look after myself."

"You'll need to with that lot." And this time Sonny's voice was sharp. "You might live to regret it." Rob frowned and then smiled. If he never saw her again he would never regret meeting Amelia.

He worked steadily through the day, taking the ribbing from his friends about his promotion with good heart. He made up his mind to write and let the Craddocks know about his promotion. He thought they would be pleased. The tailor stitched on his chevron and there was no doubt that he felt proud as he viewed himself in the mirror before leaving for town.

Sonny came up behind Rob and placed a hand upon his shoulder. "Look, mate, I don't want to keep on about this, but why not come along with us to the *Shamrock*. Give the high life a miss."

Rob shrugged abruptly. "I'm a big boy now, Sonny. I'm telling you, see to your own business. He felt that they were only jealous because such a beauty as Amelia had taken a fancy to him. And she must have done, otherwise she wouldn't have stayed with him all evening. They could look for their own women, he was going back to find Amelia.

Turning, he flicked Sonny's ear. "I'm on a winner this time, old boy. A real winner."

CHAPTER 10

Rob marched through the barrack gates and then, once out of sight, walked with the brigade swagger down the streets towards the West End. His eyes shone and his face was wreathed in a wide smile at the thought of the evening ahead. Several young girls gave him the gladeye and he laughed back at them and twirled his moustache invitingly. But they could see he was not seriously trying to pick them up. His thoughts were with Amelia. She was a real lady and no mistake.

Deciding to take a tram, he sat on the open top deck and looked around the busy streets. Lights shone in the dusky gloom of the autumn evening and the effect was like a giant Christmas tree. Crowds thronged the streets again, some the worse for wear, others walking haughtily arm in arm, skirting around the beggars who stood on almost every street corner. They wailed tuneless songs or just stood there with hands out, begging for the odd copper or two.

Rob leapt off the tram and, feeling in a generous mood, tipped a tanner into the bag of an old woman standing with a few withered blooms.

"That's decent of you, soldier. Here, take this lot and good luck to you. She bent down and from a basket hidden under the black voluminous skirts, drew out a small fresh posy of three red rose buds. "The last rose of summer. Here, take them for your lady love."

Rob smiled and took the posy. They would be the finishing touch. It made him look a proper gent to take a lady flowers. He couldn't really believe it was him. He was smart, had money in his pocket, and was buying flowers for an actress in the West End of London. It was a long way from the soot boy. What would his father have thought? He would probably have tried to cadge some money, but Rob would have liked his mother and his sister Mary to see him now.

The theatre was packed again with people standing at the back, singing and swaying in rhythm. Rob settled down into his seat and waited for the curtains to rise. He searched up and down the line of high kicking chorus girls for Amelia. Was it her night off? He realised that he would look a right fool after all his bragging if she wasn't there.

The mood changed as the lights dimmed and, dressed as a dream in white and pink satin, Amelia stood on stage. She smiled shyly and fluttered her eyelashes. Rob's heart swelled with pride. Her voice, although not strong, was sweet enough to still the audience into a hush as she sang, "Oh my love is like a red, red rose that's newly sprung in June." She roamed the stage expertly, going into every corner and looking up into the gallery and boxes. Rob's throat tightened as she sang, "And I will love thee still my love, till all the seas run dry." He sighed, thinking, if only she would, if only she could.

The applause was deafening. She was nothing out of the ordinary, but she had a beauty and presence that held the audience in the palm of her hand, "Encore — Encore" they roared and Rob joined in with them and stood and clapped as they egged her on.

Clearly feeling more assured, she sang again with more power and feeling, going down the catwalk into the audience. Rob daringly threw his posy which she caught. She smiled straight at him, but gave no sign of recognition. Stepping back onto the stage she blew him a kiss and his heart flew as high as a bird.

In the interval he went to the bar and found her there talking intently to a tall, well-built man. He looked much older than Amelia and Rob presumed that it was her boss and decided not to interrupt them. She saw him and half smiled. Boldly he went over and, touching his hat, said, "Good evening, miss. You did well tonight."

"Who's the boy then?" asked the man with a wave of his arm.

Amelia shrugged her shoulders and Rob explained, "We met the other night, miss, at the pub around the corner with my mates." She looked a little vague and Rob made to move away and make his excuses, but the man held on to his arm.

"You're not interrupting soldier. Here, you stick around and keep Amy company. It's time I was off."

Amy leaned forward and held onto his arm. "You'll come back, Jack, after the show?"

"Can't, old dear. Another client to see." He took his leave hurriedly as if he couldn't wait to get away.

Amy sighed and turned her attention to Rob. "Gin, soldier, a large one. Mother's ruin," she laughed, her face twisted bitterly.

"You all right, miss. Nothing wrong I hope?" Rob asked.

"Oh no, soldier, nothing wrong. Nothing that would interest you." And she downed the drink in one gulp. "Stage fright, always affects me this way," she smiled at him. "Another large one soldier."

"Do you think you should miss. Are you on in the second half?"

"Don't tell me what to do, soldier. If you can't get me a drink, somebody else will."

Rob did as she asked and after taking this one more slowly, she seemed to calm down. The bell sounded for the second act, and Amy left. "See you after the show, Miss Amelia?" he asked hesitantly.

"Amy, they call me Amy. And, yes, if you want to," she answered.

In the second act, Amy played the support to the juggling act and as soon as she entered the side of the stage, Rob could see that she had obviously been drinking more. She stumbled and the juggler tried to laugh it off as she misaimed the three coloured hoops which fell in a jumbled heap. "Feeling all right dearie, or is it stage fright?" he laughed.

Amy ignored him and proceeded to take everything off the table and throw it at him with no aim at all. The clubs hit the board, and the balls went across the stage and into the audience who went wild and clapped and cheered at what they thought to be a comedy act. The juggler tried hard to cover up and at first he went along as if it really was part of the act. But Amy then reached for the knives and proceeded to throw them at the board. The juggler ducked and stage hands rushed on to help then, seeing the flying knives, rushed off and hid behind the props as the shining blades hurtled through the air.

Rob couldn't stand any more and leaping on to the stage, he swept Amy up in his arms. For a minute she struggled, kicking her legs and almost knocking him out. His hat fell to one side over his eye and she lifted it and kissed him fully on the mouth. The audience roared in appreciation.

"Come to my rescue have you, soldier. Come to rescue little old Amy?"

Rob stalked off the stage and into the wings. "Take her round the back, the silly bitch. Here, you can leave her now, lad. I'll see to her." An elderly woman came towards Rob and led him to a narrow alleyway between the scenery where a couch stood against the wall. "Chuck her on there. I've told her many times, but will she listen? Will she hell as like."

The old woman seemed familiar, but Rob was too intent on his task to worry about that. He laid Amy down gently. "Does she do this often then, missus?" he asked.

"Too bloody often, soldier, too bloody often. Here, come on gel, pull yourself together." Amy stirred and then fell back. "Leave her here a bit, she'll come round before the show's done. You get back and enjoy yourself."

Rob didn't want to do that. He wanted to stay. He looked up at the old woman and remembered where he had seen her. She was the old flower seller. "Here, you sold me the roses a while ago, remember?"

The old woman smiled. "Aye, I saw them in her room."

Rob heard the words but he didn't care. A beauty like Amy was bound to have dozens of admirers. "You all right now, miss? Come along and I'll get us home."

"Stop calling me miss, soldier. I'm Amy, and where's home?"

"Why, to your place, mis.. Amy. Come along now. I'll get us a cab."

Amy allowed Rob to support her and they left by the stage door. A cab waited down a side street and Rob whistled him down.

"My, you must be flush," she laughed and clambered into the cab. "You married, or anything?" she asked as they faced each other in the darkness.

"No, nor spoken for either," he smiled.

"Come here then, come and give us a cuddle." She was still half drunk, but Rob was not one to miss an opportunity like this and he went to her side. Taking her in his arms, he kissed her passionately. She responded with equal passion and they came to earth with a jolt as the cabbie drew up outside a large double-fronted house with bay windows.

"This is home, soldier. The Bradford Lodging House. Paying guests a speciality, and too ruddy true. A speciality 'cos they very rarely get any."

Rob led her to the front door and made to salute in farewell. "Oh, no you don't, soldier. Come on in. Let's have a little natter." He followed her readily.

The room was pleasant enough, adequately furnished and clean, but with a smell of stale drink about it.

"Do you all live here then?" he asked. She shook her head. "Only two of us, me and Maggy. We both come from Bradford you see, come down to make our fortunes and find a rich husband from the stage door Johnnies. That's a laugh." She poured him a whisky and herself another gin and they talked.

Amy had come to London after being told that her dancing and singing were bound to make her a star, only they hadn't. "There's thousands like me in this city, thousands. I'm no better than most," she sighed.

"Yes you are. To me you are, Amy," said Rob eagerly.

"You really mean it, don't you soldier?" Then, holding him in a passionate embrace, she began to fondle him. Rob needed no arousing. He had loved her from the moment he had set eyes on her. They made love for what seemed like hours and then finally both fell asleep.

It was dawn before he awoke to find her standing over him with a cup of tea in her hand. "Come on, soldier, time to leave. Here, get this down you and be off."

Rob stared at her. "Be off? I ain't going anywhere. At least I am going back to camp, but I'm coming back tonight. I'm not leaving you, Amy. I'm not a one night stand, my girl. No fear."

Amy stared at him. "You what?"

"I'm coming back tonight."

"Like hell you will. You're just like all the rest, soldier. Here, give us ..." she stopped and stared again at him. "You really mean it, don't you?"

Rob nodded. "If you want me to prove it, I'll stay all day. I'll get put on orders, but that'll be all right and we can stay in or go for a walk. A bit of fresh air will do you good."

Amy sat down and started to sob uncontrollably. "I've never met a bloke like you, Rob. 'Sakes alive, I thought you were like all the rest. Here, come and give us a kiss." She held out her arms and Rob picked her up and twirled her round the room.

"I'm going to be around for a long time Amy my girl, for ever if you'll let me."

"You mean that?"

"Yes, my little mor, I mean it," said Rob as he lapsed back into his Suffolk brogue.

She kissed him again and his heart flooded with love for this beautiful creature. "What shall we do now then?" she laughed.

"Let's get wed." The words came out without thinking, but he had no regrets.

"Wed? You mean married? Don't be daft."

"I'm not being daft, I mean it. Will you marry me?"

"Really? Well, if that's what you want soldier, yes I'll marry you."

Rob whooped with joy and almost threw her into the air. They fell laughing onto the bed and then, realising the seriousness of the moment, sat staring at one another in awe. "Should we stay in and discuss the future. Do you want to be a soldier's wife?"

"Never thought about it, but I guess it's as good as being anybody else's wife. Come on, get dressed, soldier. If we are to be wed, I don't want you in trouble with the army. We'll go back to the barracks. I'll ride with you and then we'll meet again tonight. I'll come over there as we don't have a show tonight."

"I don't want you to go back to the theatre," said Rob. "I can keep you. You can stay here and we'll get wed as soon as we can. It need only be a few weeks and then we'll have the allowances. You give that job up and I'll take care of you. You'll be missis Rob Clamp before you know it."

She rolled the name around on her tongue. "Funny, I never thought about your name. Mine is Amelia Pressure, Amy for short."

"Pressure. I'll call you precious. My Amy precious." Rob smiled tenderly. He had never felt like this before. His only love had been the army, and he was sure that Amy would make a great army wife.

She dressed in a smart grey costume with high heeled shoes and as they travelled to the barracks, he felt like a king. Her golden hair was coiled around her cheeks and she wore a pink feathered hat, jauntily perched upon the curls.

"You are beautiful, really beautiful," said Rob as she smiled and nestled at his side on the top deck of the bus. She swayed as the horses set off at a gallop. "You all right, gel?" he asked.

"Yes, yes I'm fine. Just a bit giddy. All this excitement is too much for me in one day."

"You look pale. Here, rest your head on my shoulder."

They arrived near the barracks and she appeared to be glad to get off. Her cheeks were flushed and yet her skin was pale. Rob put it down to all the late nights she had at the theatre, but that would soon be over. At the gates he kissed her on the cheek and saluted. "You be here tonight, gel, at six o'clock sharp," he ordered and she nodded and waved as the big doors closed behind him.

As he entered the block his mates began to tease him. "Oh aye then, old Rob, where you been? Found a good lodging have we?"

Rob threw his hat on the bed and sat down. "Fancy being my best man?" he asked Sonny.

"What?" Sonny roared.

"Best man. I'm getting wed, to that stage lady." He chose his words carefully.

"You fool, you bloody fool. Why she's no more than..."

Rob swung his fist and sent Sonny reeling across the room and into a locker. Sonny stood up and wiped the blood pouring from his mouth. "I don't give a damn if you kill me. You're a bloody fool and I'll not see you hang yourself with the likes of her. I'd be no mate if I did. You'll regret it. You can get another best man."

"Oh no, I won't regret it mate. You wait and see," Rob snarled. He was angry with himself for hitting his friend and angry with his friend for slanging Amy. What had they got against the girl? They didn't even know her, but he could see Sonny was upset about something. He went to help his friend to his feet and offering his hand said, "Sorry mate, but you shouldn't say things like that. If you knew her you'd think differently. Come with me tonight and meet her properly, you and Walt. How about that?" His two mates looked at one another. "If you call yourself mates, real mates..." Rob was getting angry again.

"You're right. Aye, I'll stand for you, and you'll come along and all, won't you Walt, and see this silly bugger hang himself?" said Sonny and the three shook hands and jostled each other happily.

After his guard duty Rob sat down and wrote to the Craddocks. "Dear Sergeant and Missus. I would like you to make arrangements to come along to London and meet my intended and also attend the wedding. Would you, if possible, let my sister Mary know and I will let you know the date as soon as I can. And oblige, Rob Clamp. CPL."

There, that made it almost official. He would have to see the C.O. and get all the details worked out, but his mates were coming, and he was sure that the Craddocks and Mary would come as well. He would talk over the rest of the arrangements with Amy tonight.

Rob desperately wanted to write to his mother and let her know as well and decided to send a note, and a bit of money, to the vicar. He would love to know what she would think of him getting married, and to such a lady and all.

Outside the barrack gates Amy stood waiting, tight black skirt just above the ankles topping pearl buttoned boots. His Amy, his wife. The thought of her belonging to him almost choked the breath from his body. Amy Clamp — the name had a real ring to it!

CHAPTER 11

The wedding took place in the military chapel four weeks later on a misty November morning. Amy looked beautiful in a blue flowered dress under a velvet coat. "They gave it to me from the wardrobe at the theatre," she told Rob in explanation of his question as to the coat.

Nobody had tried to stop her leaving the theatre and had indeed been very helpful, with old Mrs. Lambert, the flower woman making a cake and Jack Warrick, her agent, making a nice cash donation, "To give the young 'uns a bit of a start," as he said.

Being settled and not working the long hours had brought a bloom to her cheeks and she had put on a bit of weight. Rob had spent many happy hours in her lodgings, but they were to live in the barracks in a two-up two-down house that backed onto the square. "Look, it's all furnished, right down to the pots and pans. Couldn't ask for more could we now?" Rob had said and, smiling, Amy shook her head.

Rob was nervous about the meeting with the Craddocks and Mary who had made arrangements to attend the wedding. Sergeant Craddock had written and asked if he was sure and was it a "forced do". But Rob didn't even bother to reply. He was in heaven.

It was a full military wedding, with all the male guests in uniform. Mary had got herself well done up and he felt very proud as he met her with the Craddocks outside the church. "You ain't done nothing wrong have you our Rob?" Mary asked.

Rob laughed. "Well, I ain't going to say that exactly, but we ain't getting off to a bad start if that's what you mean."

And then Amy arrived with some of her theatrical friends and they entered the church. There were no frills to the ceremony, no hymns or walking down the aisle, just a simple ceremony and reception at the good old *Shamrock* who put on a decent spread of cold ham and cakes.

"This is the new Mrs. Clamp then?" the sergeant said and held out his hand to Amy.

"I've heard such a lot about you. Rob is very proud of you and your wife," replied Amy, and leaning forward gave them both a gentle kiss on the cheek.

"I told you she was a winner, didn't I?"

Sergeant Craddock wrinkled his nose and said nothing. Mary

stood in awe. She had never seen anything as beautiful or as fragile as Amy. "You know how to feed our Rob, then?" was all she could think of to ask.

Amy's laugh tinkled through the room. "Feed him? That depends on what he wants. We've been living on love these past few weeks, ain't we love?" Rob blushed and smiled.

Walt and Sonny did a marvellous job throughout the day, mixing with Amy's friends and making a real fuss of Mary and the Craddocks, especially Sonny who seemed taken with Rob's sister.

The drink flowed freely and Amy and all her friends got drunk. Rob was quite merry and thoroughly enjoyed himself. After all it wasn't every day that a fellow got married, he thought, it was a once in a lifetime thing.

As the day ended Sergeant Craddock suggested to Rob that he take his wife home. "We've got to get going now lad and I reckon Amy's well ready for bed."

"You like her though, don't you Sergeant. I've done well for myself?"

Always honest, Sergeant Craddock answered slowly, "I hope so lad, I hope so."

Sonny and Walt decided that they would carry the bride and groom to their little house and, picking up Amy, Sonny charged off, with Walt carrying Rob over his shoulder through the streets until they finally deposited them on their front doorstep. "There you are. And don't do anything I wouldn't," Sonny laughed and patted Rob on the shoulder.

Amy clung to Rob as he opened the door and he had to carry her upstairs. There would be no honeymoon lovemaking for him. Amy was too drunk, but he didn't care. She was his now and they'd have plenty of time for everything.

The months passed quickly. Rob got on well and was in line for another promotion, but it would mean him going for a tour of duty in Ireland.

"How would you like that gel?" he asked. Amy tilted her head to one side and after a pause said, "Don't think so Rob. Mucky old Ireland, all taties and farming. No, you go and I'll stay here. It won't be for long will it.?"

Rob was disappointed, but on the advice of Sergeant Craddock and his C.O. decided to go. It would mean more pay and Amy was always going on that they were hard up, too hard up to go out every night. Often, if he was on duty, she would go up the West End to see her theatre friends and, once or twice, she had stopped overnight with Mrs. Lambert. "Gives me a bit of life, love, keeps me going," she told him. But she was loving, kept the house clean and made good meals, what more could he want?

It was an exciting time to be in London. The Queen was about to celebrate her Diamond Jubilee and the festivities would last well over a week. There was to be dancing and street parties and all would be climaxed by a big parade in which the Queen herself would drive through her capital city. Amy was planning to spend every day up in town. The theatres were alive with songs and ditties and squads of soldiers could be seen everywhere, marching and drilling.

It fell to Rob's company to form part of the mounted bodyguard. He was so proud and as Corporal of the guard, he deemed it a great honour. It seemed to be a culmination of his career. He decided to write and let his mother know and sent it as usual through the vicar. He gave all his news and added that he would love her to see him at the Jubilee. "London wouldn't suit her, lovey, she'd be lost," Amy had said and, of course, she was right. But a week before the parade, Rob got a letter from his sister telling him that she was making arrangements to bring his mother to London.

She wrote, "I've been writing to Sonny many times and it would be nice to see him again. Don't worry about the money. I'm in good work now as barmaid and cook down at the pub in Stowmarket. It's good money and I don't spend much so I'll see to all she wants. Just make sure you're there to make her welcome."

Rob was so excited. How many years was it since he had seen his mother? What would she wear? He had only seen her in old shawls and skirts. His father had never bothered much about looks. He was much too keen on the drink. And she had never been on a train before. Would she stand up to it all? These thoughts went round and round in his mind. He was excited and apprehensive. He asked Amy what she thought of it all and she shrugged and said she hoped she would be in to make them a cup of tea.

"Why, where are you going?" Rob asked.

"Well, with all this lot going on, I'll more than likely be up town. I've made arrangements to meet the girls and lads. You'll be on duty most of the time and you don't want me stuck here on my own do you?"

For once, Rob lost his temper. "I want you here to meet my

mother. She's coming a long way and she's an old woman and I want her made welcome."

"Well, let her come. I'll leave the key and they can make themselves a drink."

"But it's my mother Amy, my old lady. I ain't seen her for years, not since I ran away from home. And you ain't never seen her. Don't you want to meet my family?"

"Not really. Not after what you've told me about them. Your old man sounds a right old bugger, and as for the rest of them, it must be like a bleeding workhouse." Her voice was peevish and it was obvious she was not interested in his mother, but Rob would not let the matter drop.

"I want you here, you hear me now Amy?" his voice was strong and firm.

"Well, I ain't going to be here my lad. I'm off up to town like I said, and bugger your old lady. She sounds a right pain to me. Who but an idiot would put up with what she does, aye, tell me that?"

Rob went wild. "My mother is a bloody angel compared to you and if you ain't here to meet her I'll — I'll..." He raised his arm threateningly, but managed to stop himself before the blow was struck.

"Go on, hit me then, you big brave soldier. Show us what a man you are," Amy sneered and braced herself up to him. His reaction was to grab her roughly and kiss her passionately. "You drive me wild sometimes Amy. I don't know what to make of you, but I know one thing, you be here to meet my mother, right?" His voice held the authority of the army orders and she could see that he was angry in a cold, controlled way.

Amy didn't want the bother of a row. Life with Rob was fairly easy. She kept him happy and she was left, through his long hours of duty, very much to her own devices and that was how she liked it. She had the best of both worlds — a secure life with Rob, a bit of money in her pocket, a full belly, no pressures, and she could spend time with her show business friends. So she kissed him softly and whispered that he was not to worry, she wouldn't let him down.

The day before the celebrations all military personnel had to report for duty at three o'clock. Uniforms had to be pressed, buttons, helmets and breastplates polished. Rob, Walt and Sonny revelled in it all. They were to be on mounted guard in full dress and although they had done many city parades, this was the first major one to include royalty.

That night the barrack doors were locked and every man was more or less under house arrest with no drinking. They had to get some sleep for the long day ahead and see that everything was in tip-top condition.

Rob slept fitfully. He had a nagging worry at the back of his mind that would not let him rest. "Sonny, Sonny, here mate give us a hand. I'm off home for a minute."

"No you bloody aren't. You're stopping here."

"I have to go home I tell you. Something's wrong. I've got a feeling."

Sonny could see that he was deadly serious and went and wakened Walt. "The silly bugger wants to go home to see things are all right. It's no good going on at him, he's made his mind up. We'd best give him a hand."

The doors were barred and bolted so there was no way out there. The windows were high, but with a bit of contriving they stood like acrobats on each other's shoulders until Rob could manage to pull himself up and open the bottom window. He heaved himself up and jumped lightly onto the barrack square. He paused and looked around at the shadows cast by the eerie gaslight. He shivered and then sped across the yard and round the back to the houses. He was amazed that nobody challenged him, but they would never think of anyone wanting to get out on a night like this.

The house was in darkness and Amy would be asleep, but yet the feeling lingered, making him afriaid that all was not well. He tapped softly on the door and called out her name. There was no answer. He did not want to enter the house and frighten her, that would be daft, but after several minutes of calling, nothing happened. His foreboding increased and he decided to go in. He couldn't afford to wait any longer or he would be missed and then they would all be in trouble.

Gently he placed the key in the lock and opened the door. Standing at the foot of the stairs he called out her name. "Amy — Amy?" There was no reply. With fear in his heart, he leapt up the stairs two at a time and pushed open the bedroom door. His breath choked in his throat. The bed was empty, and had not even been slept in. Where was she? Hurriedly he went through the house, looking in all the cupboards. Her clothes were still there so she hadn't left him.

He sat on the bed and then decided to go back to the barracks. There was nothing more that he could do. Perhaps she was just late home? He looked at the clock and saw that it was almost eleven, but the streets would be crowded and she would have had a job getting home. Feeling more reassured, he made his way back and arrived at the high window. How was he going to get up there? He hadn't thought of that.

"Sonny, are you there mate?"

"'Course we bloody are. Where the hell have you been?"

Rob laughed at the familiar voice. "How do I get back in?"

"How do I know?" came the reply.

"Get the sheets, knot them, chuck them through the window and I'll drag myself up."

"Bloody Houdini, that's what you are." But they did as Rob said and as the blankets came through the window he dragged himself up and was just about to put this leg through the window when soft applause came from the square.

"Well done, Corporal Clamp. Going into the circus are we?" It was an officer and the duty sergeant.

Rob stopped and with feet balanced on the sill held himself against the window with the blanket. He tried to stand to attention and then laughing said, "Sir, I was just demonstrating how to ascend Nelson's column if we need to get anyone down tomorrow. Some might get a little tiddly, Sir , you never know." The men in the square laughed and then went about their duties.

"You jammy bugger. If it had been us, we'd have been on jankers now," his friends said as he climbed through the window.

"You ain't got my charm have you?"

"Well?" Sonny asked.

"Well what?"

"You know well what. What's up?"

"Nothing. I was just being daft." And Sonny could see that the subject was closed as far as Rob was concerned. He shrugged and went back to his bunk.

The next morning, in all their finery, they trotted out in columns to line the streets. Wives, children and mates had gathered at the gates to wave them off. Some had union jacks in their hands and others shouted words of praise. Rob looked for Amy, half-heartedly knowing that she would not be there; but he could hope.

The parade settled into position and they all took their places. On the word of command, swords were drawn in salute and as Rob obeyed, he heard a voice cry out, "That's my boy, that's my little old Robbie, my boy."

He could not turn, but he knew it was his mother and from the corner of his eye he could see her with Mary. She was wearing a coat, a hat and looked so small with her grey hair drawn back from her brown weatherbeaten face. Tears came to his throat and he could not stop them from coursing down his cheeks as he saw her push towards him still saying, "It's my boy," and then go on to tell the person nearby, in her broad Suffolk brogue, that she had not seen him since he joined the army as an apprentice. "He's over six feet now my Mary says. My word, his father would be proud, wouldn't he Mary? And my Mary, she's going to marry Rob's friend and they're going to take a pub."

Rob could hear all this in the background and Mary tried desperately to hush his mother, but she would have none of it. She told of the train journey, of going to a cafe, and how the vicar's wife and the lady mistress up at the hall had rigged her out for the day. "And we're going to his house for tea later. That'll be a do. I ain't seen his wife, a rare beauty by all accounts. Oh, I'm that fussed." And she broke down and cried. Rob could not resist turning and he saw that his mother's hat was all askew as she waved and shouted. When the Queen came by his mother stopped and stared in wonderment as the parade gave the salute and the Queen bowed in acknowledgement. "You see that Mary, she smiled at our Rob." Excitement and the marvel of the occasion overcame her and she once again stood and sobbed.

Mary put her arm around her mother and cried with her. And for Rob, the tough lad from Suffolk, it also became too much and, although he was still at attention, he cried unashamedly.

CHAPTER 12

It was a wonderful day. The crowds danced in the streets after the procession had passed. They had waved and shouted at their beloved queen and they had cried as they saw the tiny figure bowing in acknowledgement. Rob was doubly delighted: first, for being on parade for such an anniversary and then because after all these years, he could see his mother again.

Back at the barracks he stabled his horse and carried out his duties as quickly as he could before signing out to go home. He prayed Amy would be there and as he approached the house and no one was waiting outside, he gave a silent thank you. Amy must be home. He entered and shouted, "You there my dear?"

The answer came from Mary who appeared at the kitchen door with teapot in hand. Rob looked at her. "What's up. Amy not here then? How did you get in?" the words tumbled out of him.

"She's here all right. She's upstairs sleeping it off."

Rob's colour rose. "You mean she's drunk?"

"Not exactly. A bit worse for wear. Evidently she's been up the West End since yesterday afternoon. They stayed up all night at the theatre having a party."

"Where's mother?" Rob asked.

"She's in the front room. She has been round the house twice. It's like a mansion to her."

Rob went in and with a forced smile swept the tiny figure into his arms and hugged her.

"Here, you put me down you daft old bor. You ain't too big for me to give you a good hiding yet you know."

But he held her tightly for a time, smelling the old familiar sage with which she washed her hair. "You're littler than ever, you work too hard, you know that?"

She laughed at him and slid to the floor, looking up at him in breathless wonder. "You're the biggest of the lot. Harry's a fair size and Albert and all, but you, you must be more'n six feet. My, you've changed." The pride rang in her voice. "It was a good day's work you did joining the army young Rob Clamp, the best day's work you ever did."

"I'm sorry about Amy..," began Rob.

His mother put up her hand to stop the flow of words. "Don't bother yourself bor. I've lived with this sort of thing all my married life. Let's just have a cup of tea and a bite to eat. I'll see Mrs. Clamp when she gets round to herself." She emphasised the word "Mrs." with some bitterness.

Mary set the table for tea and it was evident that she had done some shopping for there were cakes and sandwiches and biscuits to eat. They ate, chatting away and catching up with all the gossip of home. Not much had changed. Most of his mates were married and some had children.

"You having a family then bor?" his mother asked.

Rob had never thought about that. A family? Well, he just might if Amy was in the mind. He leaned back and looked across at his mother. "Life any easier then, me old mor?" he asked.

Mother laughed. "Life's never been easy bor, and don't you forget it. If it were, we'd not appreciate it, would we?"

Amy still did not appear and he didn't want the bother of rousing her and provoking a row so he saw his mother and sister to the station alone. Kissing his mother tenderly, he pushed a pound note into her pocket. "Here, get yourself something with that." With tears in her eyes, she leaned out of the carriage window, waving until Rob was just a dark spot on the horizon.

Rob walked home very slowly, not knowing what he would find when he got there. He wished life could be normal, with Amy waiting with a cup of tea and a meal, or just waiting. He could hear her singing as he opened the door. "It's only me," he called.

"What do you mean only me. You're the most important thing in my life," she answered and entwined herself around his body.

"That's why you got drunk and forgot about my mother coming then? Because I'm so damned important?"

She ruffled the hair at the base of his neck. "I was tired, that's all. I went up town early last night to get a good place for the gang. We saw it all, it was wonderful, and then we had a drink and with not eating and being tired out, I just flaked."

"Did you see me then?"

She smiled. "Of course I did."

"Where did you stand?"

That stumped her. "Oh, I don't know. I just stood and you were across the road."

Rob had to take her word for it. "'Come on, let's have a cup of tea. I want to talk to you." His voice was firm.

"I could think of other things to do than talk," she whispered, but this time he did not take any notice.

"Come on, let's be sensible. Now, you know I've been on about Ireland. Well, I reckon we ought to go. It'll give us a chance to get a bit of money together and then we can maybe think on starting a family."

She stared at him. "I ain't ever thought about that Rob. I don't fancy squealing brats around the place, and besides, think on my figure."

"To hell with your figure. I'm going to put in for the posting first thing and you're coming with me, got it?"

Amy could see it was no use arguing. Rob had made his mind up that this was one way to get her away from the theatre and maybe get some semblance of organised life. After stables next morning he asked to see his Commanding Officer and put in the application. He was surprised to see that Sonny was also waiting for an interview.

"Well, I might as well tell you, only Mary said not to say anything until it was all settled. We're getting married. I'm coming out. I've done twelve years and I can sign on for eight years reserve. With the pension and my bit of money we're going to take a pub down the West End. I'm putting in for a discharge when my time is up in three months. Is that all right Rob, I never thought to ask?"

Rob shook his hand. "It's fine by me, mate. I couldn't think of anyone better for our Mary. I hope everything goes all right for you both."

"Well, you'll be at the wedding anyway. You'll see how things go."

Rob told him that he was not likely to be there as he was putting in for the Ireland posting.

"You're wise there, Rob. It'll do you both the world of good to get away on your own."

"What about Walt then. What's he going to do?" Rob asked.

"Would you believe it, he's putting in for promotion. Going on a course to make an officer I'm told." Rob smiled at this news. Well, they were all finally parting to go their different ways.

Amy was not pleased with the news and made no bones about it. "Ireland is a funny old place. What am I going to do there. I'll not have any friends and nobody to mix with. What am I supposed to do?"

"Be a bloody wife like the others and mix with them," Rob snapped.

The next few weeks were a strain. Amy did exactly as Rob told her and started to pack. She did not go up west so often and she provided meals and made life as comfortable as she could without giving away too much affection.

One morning about five o'clock, he woke to find her retching in the kitchen sink. "You caught something then?" he asked as he struggled into his trousers, trying to bring the braces over his shoulders and hold her head at the same time.

"No. I reckon I'm pregnant."

"What?" he shouted, jumping back and looking at her.

"Expecting. Well, that's what you wanted isn't it?"

Rob whooped with joy and picked her up and kissed her gently on the mouth.

"Don't do that, I feel rotten. And anyway, that's put paid to your plans hasn't it. I can't go to Ireland now, can I? I ain't going over that bloody water feeling the way I do. And I want my baby born in a hospital here, properly."

Rob thought for a moment and a doubt crept into his mind. "You're sure that's what it is? You ain't been boozing again?"

Amy sighed. "Course I know. Women know these things. But don't let it change your plans. You go off to Ireland and I'll stay here until the baby's born and then either I'll join you or you come back."

"You seem to have got it all planned," he said.

She brushed aside his doubts and said it was the only thing to do under the circumstances. "They'll let me stop here. You'll be posted here again and it would be daft to do anything else. I can come over and visit and you'll get leave. It won't be for long, Rob."

And he had to believe her. What else could he do? It was a tearful farewell as he left to catch the boat train. Amy cried and clung to him saying that she would miss him and what would she do without him.

"You take care of yourself, that's all my girl. See you and that baby of mine is kept fine and dandy." And he was on his way.

Amy was right. Ireland was not the place of plenty, but it was green, lush green, and the beer was the best that Rob had ever tasted. The life was poor but good. The barracks had plenty to eat and they mixed with the townsfolk of Currah who were glad of the extra money brought in by the army. Some were hostile and Rob couldn't blame them. It was their country after all. Time had no meaning. Amy wrote now and again with all the news and he wrote back, but there wasn't much to tell.

One morning he was summoned to the Colonel's office and was told he was going on leave that weekend. "Your child's about due is it not Clamp?" Rob answered, "Yes sir." "Well, you've got a whole week. I hope the little beggar makes it whilst you're home."

He really did not have time to let Amy know that he was coming and decided to surprise her on arrival. He bought some linen things for the baby and a pure silk blouse for Amy to take back with him. It would be nice to see the old place again and he thought of the tightknit community of the barracks and especially of Sonny and Walt. But they were no longer there. Six months ago Sonny and Mary had got married and Walt had gone off to Norfolk on a course. However, the thought of Amy was enough. It would be great to have a whole week with her at home.

He arrived to an empty and locked house. Surely she wasn't up to her old tricks again, not with the baby so near. He hammered twice on the door and windows and then heard a shout from behind. The duty sergeant was beckoning him into the guardroom.

"Your wife's in maternity, Clamp. Nothing too wrong, but there's just a bit of a complication it appears. Here, get yourself up there right away."

Rob needed no second telling. He dumped his bags and ran all the way to the local hospital. Arriving gasping for breath, he asked for his wife.

"Ah, yes, well you're too late." Rob stared glazedly at the nurse. "Oh, everything's all right. You've got twins that's all, a beautiful girl and boy, and not expected from what I gather."

Rob almost fainted. Twins — two of them! Well, that was a turn up. "Come along then, Corporal, follow me."

He was led up a winding corridor into a side ward where Amy lay back on the pillows looking pale but still beautiful. "Here, oh, I don't know what to say. You're a marvel, a marvel my love."

She squirmed as he tried to hold her. "Mind it Rob, I'm a bit sore. Twins ain't no joke."

"Well, we ain't got any in our lot as I know of. Where are they?"

Amy pointed to two canvas cribs in which lay his son and daughter. They were beautiful. He felt so proud of his family and turning, smiled at his wife. "Here, I've brought you some things. Some for the little ones and the house as well."

She hitched herself up in bed and he noticed the pure silk nightdress and matching jacket in pink trimmed with furry stuff.

"Where did you get all that finery?" he asked.

"Oh, the gang sent them for me. Two sets actually. Aren't they nice?" She spoke casually and gave only a cursory glance at his treasured gifts.

"What are we going to call them then?" he asked.

"I thought Jack and Cora, a bit stage-like should they want to follow in my footsteps and go into the theatre."

"Not if I can help it," he answered, but agreed to the names.

After leaving the hospital he decided to visit his sister Mary and Sonny. He found the pub and marched up to the bar saying in a loud voice, "Pint of mild and bitter, and be quick about it missus."

Mary was just about to give him a rude retort when she saw who it was and almost jumped back in excitement. "Sonny, Sonny, look who's here?" she cried and dragged Rob into the cosy kitchen behind the bar. "Now, come on, tell me all the news. How's things?"

"Not much news, except I've got twins now, a son and daughter if you please."

Mary sighed and then kissed her brother. "I'm glad Rob, real glad, and I hope this'll make Amy settle down a bit more. Will she be going back with you then?"

"Shouldn't think so just yet. She'll not be out of confinement afore I go back, but I'm going to make sure she's with me or I'm back here within the next few months. We're a family now."

Sonny shook his hand. He and Mary were so happy. They were comfortably off and enjoyed their life. It was a special occasion and before the night was out, the two old friends were well and truly drunk, singing away at the tops of their voices. Sonny was in the Metropolitan Police, making good progress and life was good. With a niggling feeling, Rob wished he could say the same.

Every day for that week's leave, he visited the hospital, taking his wife tit-bits and presents each time. She seemed languid and not in the least bit interested in her children.

"I reckon you ought to come to Ireland. That fresh air will do the three of you good. I'll make the arrangements and then come and fetch you. All right?" Amy shrugged her shoulders as if in agreement.

And then it was time to leave again. He took a lingering look at his children and after gently kissing his wife sadly left for Ireland. In a way he was glad to be getting back. Somehow he felt the need to be on his own and think things through. He had confided in Mary his doubts of Amy and she had reassured him by saying that Amy had had a bad time. Carrying twelve pounds and then giving birth to two was not an easy job and perhaps she was suffering from childbirth depression. Rob hoped that that was all it was.

But after his arrival back at Currah, the letters were so few that he began to worry and then drink to drown his worries. For almost six months he would watch every morning as the mail came and then dash across to see if there was one for him. In all that time he only got three letters from Amy. He finally wrote to Mary and asked her to call and see if anything was amiss. Within a week he had a reply which told him that the house looked unlived in and suggested that he get special leave to sort things out.

Rob saw his commanding officer and in two days was on the ship across the Irish Channel. The train journey took hours and he was anxious to get home. He played shove-halfpenny and cards with some other soldiers and won quite a lot of money which he decided to use on taking Amy out, maybe taking the three of them down to the sea or home to see his mother.

He could tell as his hollow footsteps marched across the yard that the house was empty. He took a cab to Mary's but she didn't know where Amy was either. She tried to calm him down, but Rob drank more than he should and decided to visit the theatre, hoping to find Amy there. Mary tried to persuade him against this, but he would not listen. "Well, don't you go and get into any trouble, Rob, and come straight back here. Are you listening?" Rob was listening and nodded in agreement.

As he approached the theatre he saw old Mrs. Lambert who greeted him with delight. "Good to see you son. Here, take a rose for the missus."

"Do you happen to know where she is then," he asked and the old girl nodded. "She's been stopping with me for a bit. Got a bit lonely with you being away. Get round there. She'll be in."

Rob's heart leapt with relief. Why hadn't he thought of that? But why had Amy not let him know where she was? He almost ran up to the house to find the door wide open. He crept up the stairs to the old room and gently pushed open the door. The children were laid in one crib, top and toe, and Amy was laid on the bed, stark naked with Jack Warrick rolling all over her.

Rob did not stop for an instant. He burst through the door, took Amy by the hair and throwing her down on the floor stuck his stirrup into her gut. He yelled and took the cringing Warrick from his hiding place under the bedclothes and threw him, in one movement, through the bedroom window, the frame and glass crashing and splintering as the body hit the pavement below. Rob grabbed the children and racing down the stairs hailed a cab and set off for Mary's. He went in the back door and, standing in the kitchen, called her name.

"Oh my good grief, what have you gone and done Rob? What are you doing with these little ones? Here, give them to me." She took the children and settled them in a large drawer from the sideboard. Rob was still standing in the doorway. "You'd best tell me what's gone on then. Here, get this down you," and she offered a large whisky which he downed in one gulp.

"I found her — I found her ..." The words would not come out and tears choked his voice.

"Sit down, my dear," and Mary led him to a chair.

"I think he'd best stand up." Sonny's voice came from the doorway. He was in uniform and accompanied by another constable and sergeant. "I reckoned we'd find you here Rob."

Mary paled. "What — what have you done?"

Rob's head sank into his hands and he sobbed uncontrollably. "Are they dead?"

"Damn nearly. Anyway, to business," and the customary caution was given to Rob before the arrest was made.

Sonny stepped forward and put his hand on Rob's shoulder. "Might I say something sergeant? Can we take this man into military custody. He's a good bloke. He won't do a runner and his record is second to none. The army won't be any too pleased if we don't let them know about about all this."

The sergeant agreed and Rob sighed with relief. Turning to Mary he said, "Can you keep the little ones or take them to mother? I don't want anyone else getting their hands on my children. Can you have them?"

He looked beseechingly at Sonny who smilingly said, "Don't bother about that Rob. We'll see to the bairns. I'm coming with you now and we'll go along to the barracks and inform the colonel. He'll take over from there. Come along now."

Mary hugged her brother tearfully, but Rob smiled at her. "Just you see to them bairns. No one, and I mean no one is to have them except you, you hear now?" His voice rose as they led him away, the once proud young soldier, now shoulders dropping and head hung low.

"Come along now, Corporal Clamp. Set 'em an example. Straighten up and take your medicine," encouraged Sonny.

Rob straightened up and marched to the waiting Black Maria. At that minute he had no regrets and didn't really care if they were both dead. He had nothing to live for without Amy. How could she have done it to him and in front of the bairns too? That, and other thoughts raced through his mind.

"Penny for them?" said Sonny.

"They aren't worth a damn. Nothing's worth a damn any more."

CHAPTER 13

For three days Rob was kept in the local station. He appeared before the magistrates the next morning and was remanded in order that a report might be made by the army to take him over. His colonel turned up and spoke highly of his character in the army. Somehow, Sergeant Craddock had been told and he, too, turned up with his wife to speak on Rob's behalf. Being in the force, Sonny could not speak for him, but Mary spoke of how Rob had looked after his mother.

The most surprising thing was the fact that the two army wives who had been neighbours offered to give evidence at the trial, should it come to that. They were allowed to speak in private and told of the many visits made to Amy by gentlemen friends while Rob was on duty. They spoke of how they all seemed to be theatre gents and sometimes they brought ladies with them. Amy was also out a lot, sometimes overnight, and since Rob had been in Ireland she had stayed away, often for weeks on end, and was always being brought back by Jack Warrick, according to their description of the man. "Oh, it was all finery. A carriage and flowers, and he always carried a bottle of something," they said.

Rob sat with his head in his hands and wondered how he could have been so daft.

The application made by the army was granted and within three days he was transported to the guardroom. Whilst in the station he was treated with care and respect. Sonny was not allowed to attend him, but he was allowed to visit.

"All I want is the bairns seen to. They're my main concern," Rob said.

"Don't you want to know anything about Amy and that fellow then? One of the reasons you were kept here for three days was to see if he snuffed it or not."

"I don't give a damn. Is she all right?"

"Well, that kick didn't do her any good and she was expecting. She'll be out in a week or so. You caused a miscarriage, that's all, and a good job too. As for him, well, he's a bit broken up. His leg will be a bit shorter and his arm looks as though it won't ever straighten out again. Although you shouldn't have done it Rob, I can't say as I'm all that sorry."

"I ain't sorry about her neither. That bairn couldn't have been mine. The cow, that's what she was Sonny, a cow." Sonny touched him on the shoulder and murmured that it was all best forgotten. "I can't forget. We're still married. What shall I do now? Divorce her for adultery or what?"

"Well, she might divorce you for cruelty, or assault. Now it's in police hands you're bound to get sentenced or at least dismissed from the service."

Rob's heart sank. Everything he had dreamed of lay in ruins. After the transfer, he spent most of his time cleaning the guardroom. The colonel would not let him do the ablutions. "He's too fine a soldier for that. We must get a good case, Sergeant Major," he said. And, in spite of having his pay stopped, Rob was never short of anything. His mates and comrades brought him things to the extent that he was better off than before.

"Will they have to appear at the court martial?" he asked his defending solicitor.

"They are not fit to appear. Your wife is still rather weak and as for the man, well, it will be a long time before he is out of hospital."

"She's not my wife and never has been, if the truth be told." And never again did Rob refer to Amy other than "she" or "her".

The court martial finding was "extenuating circumstances" and Rob was sentenced to six months in gaol and then to be dismissed from the service. At this the colonel jumped to his feet and protested. "This has never been known before in the whole history of the regiment. Corporal Clamp is an excellent soldier and was provoked beyond endurance. I insist that the finding be that he is discharged from the army. He has done twelve years and has every right to an honourable discharge, although he should forego his pension. That will be punishment enough for his so called crime."

And so Rob stood stiffly to attention as the sentence was read out. Turning to his own officers he gave a text book salute and marched under close arrest to the waiting wagon which took him to the military prison. He had no regrets about what he had done. The most cruel pain was the disgrace brought to his career. As he stood on the parade ground and his chevrons were cut off his arms, he felt unshed tears pour through every fibre of his being.

Mary was allowed to see him for a few brief moments and reassured him about the children, but for his term in custody he was not allowed visitors except his solicitor who advised him to sue for divorce before Amy did. "It will save you a great deal in allowances and you have plenty of witnesses on your side." Rob shrugged and told him to get on with it.

"What are your plans?"

Again Rob shrugged. "Ain't got any. Might go home for a while. There's not much left for me to do."

"You have the children, what about them?"

"What do they want with a father like me and a mother like her. They're better off without either of us. No, my sister Mary will see to them. It's best I keep my distance." And his mind was made up.

On release he wrote to Mary and said that he was going off for a few weeks to sort himself out and he would get in touch as soon as he was ready. He looked a sight. He had no civilian clothes and the authorities had rigged him up with what was an assortment of things — grey fustian trousers, a brown jacket and a striped shirt topped with a check cap. "Talk about Joseph's coat? You look like a patchwork blanket," they laughed, but wished Rob well.

As the gates closed behind him, he felt lost. The army had taken care of everything and now he was alone. He felt like an orphan as he juggled the five shillings given to him to find temporary board and lodgings. He decided to get right away and having been given a good breakfast to send him on his road, set off towards the north, marching as if on parade.

The air felt good on his face. He breathed deeply and immediately felt better. He was on the way to a new life. The divorce was going ahead and as far as he knew, Amy was planning to marry Jack Warrick. "Good job, they deserve each other," was his only observance.

He walked for a long time, casting off first his jacket then his cap as the sun beamed it's way across the roads. He began to feel thirsty and as a farm appeared over the horizon he went towards it, knocked on the door and asked for a drink of water.

"You look a mite hot, young man. Come along in and have a drink of cold milk." The welcome was obvious from the rather well-built woman who turned out to be the farmer's wife. "The boss is down the bottom field. We're a bit short handed, what with the lads being at school. It'll be a good job when they break up. The boss is fair worn out and works from morn till night."

"Could he do with some help then?" Rob asked and she looked long and hard into his face. "I daresay he could. He'll be up in a minute. You stop and have a bite and a word with him. You look honest enough."

Rob went out into the yard and looked about him. It was clean and tidy, but you could see there was not much money around. Still, if they gave him his bed and lodging for a day or so, it would give him time to pull himself together.

The boss was a small, wiry man with twinkling eyes that looked right into Rob's soul. "You're not in trouble or ought?" he asked.

"Have been boss, nothing too serious, but I've done my punishment and I'm clear."

"Then you'd best start this afternoon after we've had dinner. Come along and set yourself down."

Rob went back into the cool kitchen and sat at the long white table. The missus served out fat bacon, mashed potatoes and cabbage. It looked nothing, but tasted so good that every morsel was like nectar. Bread and butter pudding and a mug of tea finished off the meal after which he followed the boss to the bottom field, almost a mile away, to start hedging and ditching. Rob went to work with a will and the boss could see that he was a good old country lad.

"Can't pay you much and you'll have to bed in the loft. That all right?" asked the boss.

Rob nodded. "Don't you bother about pay, just bed and feed me for a bit."

"As bad as that is it. Want to talk about it?" but Rob shook his head.

Sam and Mavis Needler turned out to be a really good Christian couple. They fed Rob well and paid him five shillings a week although they could ill afford it. After a month their sons returned and the job finished. "I can't afford to pay you any more, but you're welcome to stay awhile if you like?" Sam offered.

Rob declined and made for the nearest town of Kings Lynn and, with a few pounds in his pocket, started to look for lodgings. It was the fair weekend and Rob looked round the stalls and roundabouts.

Outside one of the booths a massive man, dressed in a skin leotard, was prancing around, sparring the air with his fists. The promoter was calling out to the young men who had gathered, challenging them to fight the man, "Battling Bill Butler is the best there is. Come along you young 'uns , have a go. Five bob if you win and a bottle of stout if you don't."

Rob looked. The bloke was big, but there was a lot of flab amongst the muscle. He was no chicken, but for this job it would be a doddle with the young lads. Battling Bill would have the expertise and skill to outwit them, but for someone who was fit, that might be something else. Rob stood amongst the crowd egging on the two young hopefuls who took the challenge and lost. And then he stepped forward and was greeted with loud laughter. He was as thin as a rake and his motley collection of clothing hung around his gaunt frame. The hard work on the farm had made him shed weight, but it had also put on the muscle and made for a lithe, lean, strong body.

He went into the corner and stripped to the waist. As the crowd saw the muscles ripple on his arms, they knew they were in for a treat. In the first round Rob played dumb and Battling Bill became cocky and clever, overplaying his skill and almost falling headlong into the large posts that supported the ring. As he turned, Rob sprang into action with a left, a right, and another left and right. Battling Bill was reeling under the blows and the promoter tried to stop the fight. Rob would have none of it. He was in for the kill and the prize was to be won. He charged forward and with a right hook landing directly under the chin, sent Battling Bill sprawling onto the makeshift canvas. Rob was the winner. The crowd cheered and, with reluctance, the promoter raised Rob's arm to declare him the winner.

In spite of the victory, he was tired. Battling Bill had put up a good fight and landed several punches which had winded Rob. He was handed the five shillings and having taken it went towards Battling Bill who was still laid out. "Come on mate, I'll give you a hand. Hope I didn't hurt you too much."

The boxer groaned, but lifted his head and, like a bolt from the blue, landed Rob a tremendous punch to the head that knocked him clean out. The crowd booed but soon dispersed as the promoter and Battling Bill carried Rob towards the caravan.

"Come on mate, that's an old trick. Thought you'd have known that one. Have a drop of this." Rob was handed a large whisky and, with his head still reeling like a top, he took a mouthful.

"Want to come with us?" the promoter asked.

Rob shook his head . "No thanks."

"Where did you learn to fight like that?" asked Bill.

"In the army."

"That's where I got mine and all. Heavyweight champion of the British Army I was. You an old sweat then?" Rob nodded and was firmly shaken by the hand.

As the promoter went away to close up for the night, Bill and Rob sat in silence and drank half a bottle of whisky between them. They were both tired, bruised and beaten.

"Ever thought about doing this sort of thing for a living? You and me could go around the booths. I'll be the manager. I'm getting too old to fight now and you can be the boy to take the challenges."

Rob thought about it before replying. "All right, it'll do for a bit anyway." They shook hands on the deal and within a few minutes Bill had packed his meagre belongings into a canvas bag and the two were on their way.

"Where to then?" Rob asked.

"Into town to old Jenny Pearson's. We'll shack up there for a couple of days and then start the round."

"What about brass?"

"I've got a bit, you'll be all right with me."

Rob was beginning to have his doubts. Boxing was all right, but no way to make a living. Still, he needed to live and to live you had to have money. "Come on then let's get going. But we'll call at the pub first and spend a bit of my winnings, your blood money Bill."

The *Blossom Tree*, was a pub that Rob would never forget. It was old, shabby, and although clean, there was sawdust on the floor and under each table a bucket was placed so that the men could relieve themselves without going outside. The stench and smoke stifled them as they entered. But the place was full and they had to edge their way along the bar to be served. The ale was good and strong and after four pints, both were just about useless.

As they left, two women approached and offered their favours. "Only a bob, mateys."

"What do you think then, Rob?" laughed Bill.

"I think they want putting in a field of stallion horses and then shooting." Rob's voice was bitter.

"You been thwarted in love then?" asked Bill.

Rob grunted and then looked at his companion. He was old and wizened and his clothes were shabby. They made a good pair as they stumbled up the road to the dingy boarding house and fell asleep into a bug-ridden bed.

Where was the soldier, the smart young brave who had only a short while ago proudly guarded the Queen? "Sod Amy, sod the bitch," he grunted bitterly into his pillow as he fell into a drunken sleep.

CHAPTER 14

For more than three long months Rob stayed with old Bill. They did the rounds of the boxing booths, making quite a good living, which they immediately drank. They slept in doss houses, rough in hedgerows or in railway sidings. Rob didn't care. He went into the ring, won most of the fights, and then looked for oblivion — anything to forget. Sometimes he vaguely thought of the bairns, but it was only fleeting. They would be all right with Mary and Sonny.

As the weeks went by he could see a change in Bill. He was getting old and no matter how bravely he tried to struggle on, his body was weakened with the strain of the blows it had taken, the lack of proper food and the vast amount of drink he must have consumed.

"How do you do it mate?" Rob asked as they settled down one night in an old clean barn near Lowestoft.

"Never knew anything else. Nearly settled down once with a lovely lady, but where could I get a job? How would I know how to work regular? This is all I've known."

Rob sighed. It looked as if it would be all he would know at this rate. His head fell forward and he drifted into a deep sleep with his head buried in a mound of soft sweet smelling hay. He dreamed of home and he saw his mother prodding away at the old copper. He even saw his father whipping the old donkey. It was a refreshing sleep which prepared him for the day to come.

An eerie silence woke him. Bill was not snoring and grunting as usual. "Bill," he whispered. "You all right mate?" The silence gave the answer. Bill had drifted into sleep and then quite peacefully, and without any pain, fallen into death.

Rob stood over the crushed and crumpled body in silent respect and then fear gripped him. What was he to do now? Should he fetch the police or just leave? But no, he couldn't do that, not to this poor old bloke. He might end up the same way.

He walked outside into the brilliant sunshine to find himself standing in a neat farm stackyard. The door of the barn opened onto rolling fields and behind the building stood a stone and red brick farmhouse. Bracing himself, and realising that he looked a horrible sight, he marched towards the farmhouse, and doffing his cap said to the young man who stood filling a white enamel pail at the well, "Good morning sir. Can you spare me a moment?" He stood back, waiting for the tirade of abuse that usually followed this request.

After all, most people thought he was a tramp, especially when Bill had been in tow, or he could be a villain, he certainly looked the part.

"Of course I can, or rather Father can. Come along inside. There may be a cup of tea and a bite to eat."

Rob was frozen to the spot. This polite, welcoming invitation inside was not expected. His eyes darted around looking for the trap.

"We aren't going to hurt you or anything. This is a Christian household and we welcome strangers. You look as though you could do with a bit of a welcome from somebody."

Rob sighed and his body relaxed as he uttered a silent prayer of thanks.

Inside the bright kitchen a girl and a woman worked at the sink and the stove. A kettle was boiling away merrily and a pot was being stirred with regular, circular movements. It was all so peaceful. He closed his eyes and was ashamed to feel a tear roll down his nose.

"Here, come on young man, don't get yourself in a state. Sit down and have a bite and a drink. Father, we've got a guest," the young man called and from a back room a large framed man entered wearing fustian trousers tied with string over boots, and the sleeves of his flannelette shirt rolled over the elbows which were bending up and down as he sharpened a long but thin carving knife on a piece of stone.

"You look done in. Sit down here. Mother, another place if you please."

Rob tried to protest, "But you don't know me. I might be anybody, a robber, murderer, anybody."

"The Lord would not send such here and if He did, then they can have all we possess if they feel they have a right to it. No, you are none of these. You look a bit down on your luck to me."

Rob nodded and sat down at the table. The girl did not speak, but smiled as she filled his plate with thick honeyed porridge covered in cream. He ate noisily and hungrily. The man placed a hand on his arm, "Take it steady. You'll be making yourself poorly, and there's plenty more." Rob eased off and finished his meal of porridge, cold fat bacon, pickles and home made bread with a large mug of strong tea.

"You like to tell us a bit about yourself then boy?"

This brought Rob up with a jolt. He had forgotten about old Bill. He stood up and beckoned to the man. "Come with me please, sir. My friend, my travelling companion, he's in the barn. We slept there last night and he.. he.. he... he died in his sleep. I found him this morning," Rob sobbed.

The woman ran and placed her arm around Rob's shaking shoulders. He couldn't understand why he was crying. He was fond of Bill all right, but not enough to behave like this.

He followed the father and son to the barn and watched as they gently laid Bill out on a canvas cover. "Looks as though he's had a rough time of it. Go back a long way some of those scars do." Rob nodded and tried, in a few broken sentences, to explain their plight.

The older man shook his head. "Well, we'll have to get this seen to. We'll leave him here for the minute. Occy, you get the trap and go along to the village and get Mr. Warner there to measure the body. "Don't you fear. We'll see to it all. The man's got to be buried. It looks as though he needs to be with the Lord. We must send him off properly, no matter what. Mr. Warner will tell Parson Judge and we'll get it done with as soon as possible. Are you his next of kin?"

Rob shrugged and explained how they had met. "I don't reckon he had anyone, so I suppose it must be me."

"That's all right then. Let's go inside and get another drink. I reckon you could do with one." And Rob did want a drink. A good strong dram would have set him up well, but he knew that this drink would be tea. At least it would refresh him and keep his wits sharp.

Within a short time it was all arranged. Bill would be buried the following day. As they gathered round the kitchen table, Rob could not believe what he was seeing or hearing. The undertaker, the parson, Occy Jordan and his father Abe, Mrs. Jordan and daughter Peggy, were all sat discussing Bill's funeral as if they were his family.

"I haven't got any money for all this," he said.

"We don't expect you have. Our poor box will pay for this job."

Rob stared. It must be a good poor box, better than home which only held the odd copper or two, a few pebbles and sometimes a bit of stale food or good paper.

"The squire helps out too, and we do have a poor relief if we need it," Mrs. Jordan tried to reassure him. "Now hymns, shall we have any?"

"Yes, I'd like the old boy to have a hymn. How about *Fight The Good Fight*. He was a boxer and a good 'un in his time. I reckon that would be fine."

The vicar tried to hide a smile but agreed that the hymn chosen would be fine. After the discussion, Rob felt out of place. He didn't know whether to walk off or to stay at the table. Jessie finally spoke to him and laughingly said, "Don't you think it's time you had a swill down? You look like a chimney sweep." Rob laughed, but without humour. Even being a chimney sweep would be better than his present state.

"Come on, I'll show you your room," and Rob was led the way up the back stairs to a tiny loft room hidden away in the corner of the eaves. It was bright and cleanly done out in cream distemper and paint. Linen curtains, made out of flour bags, hung across the window and in the corner stood a single iron bedstead with covers laid back. It looked so inviting, Rob realised how tired he felt. "I could just do with a lay down," he whispered.

Peggy laughed. "Not till you've had a wash. Mother'll kill you if you get into her clean sheets with all that dirt on you. There, get on with it," and she pointed to the washstand on the back wall which held crystal clear water, with soap on a china dish and a towel hanging on the front rail. He started to strip off. "Here, bide awhile, till I get out of the way. I don't want to see all you've got," and still laughing, she tripped happily down the stairs.

Rob slept long and deep and was awakened by a cockerel crowing in the distance. He stretched and pushed his feet to the bottom of the bed, making himself comfortable. He could hear the familiar movements of a busy house beneath him. Distant voices spoke, laughed and bantered with each other. He swung his body and placed his feet heavily on the bare wooden floor.

"Oh, you're up then?" said Mrs. Jordan, pushing open the door and peeping round. "Aye, I've had a good sleep. It was all that food you gave me. Thanks missus." "Don't thank me, boy, thank the good Lord. Here, I've brought you some of Occy's clothes. There's a shirt and some trousers. Yours are filthy and I reckon they need burning."

She tossed the garments across to him and he found she had thought of everything, even socks and a pair of boots, although how they knew his size he didn't understand. He looked to where he had left his heap of rags, but they had gone. He was glad of the fresh clean feel and smell of the new clothes and he dressed and made his way downstairs.

"Have a sup, it'll be dinner time soon, then the men will be back."

They came back sooner than expected. "Them dalled harrows, they're no good to man nor beast. We'll eat early and then Occy and me will have to go down the smithy."

"Trouble, master?" Rob asked respectfully.

"Aye. The ground's a bit rough on yon top field. We always have bother."

"Can I help? I am a smith by trade. Shall I go up and take a look."

Mr. Jordan stared into Rob's eyes. "All right. Go and see what you can do. Old Blackey's not the same since his dad died."

Rob ate quickly and then made off as directed, followed by Occy and Abe. As soon as Rob touched the set of harrows they could see that he knew exactly what he was doing. Occy fetched tools from the farm and soon they were away and working. Abe thanked Rob and offered him money which he angrily refused. "After all you've done? No, take this as part of my help for Bill's funeral."

"You can pay it in full if you stop on a bit. We've enough to keep you busy, and I know old Blackey'll be glad of a bit of help."

Rob went silent and studied his boots. It might be just the thing to get rest, regular food and a bed and a feeling of belonging again. After his army life, he missed the feeling of belonging.

"What do you say then?" Abe asked.

"Right master, I'll stop on a bit," and Rob held out his hand to Abe to shake on the deal.

Two days later Bill was buried in the tiny churchyard. Rob was the chief mourner and as they sang the words of the chosen hymn, Rob cried. He felt a hand on his arm and turning found Peggy standing at his side. She squeezed his elbow, but he made no move. Women were not yet in his programme of things. Work and health, yes, but not women, not yet and maybe not for a long time.

The days passed into months and he was happy in a vague way. They asked him questions about his life, but he only told them of his home and army life. He never mentioned Amy or the children. The blacksmith, on Abe's recommendation, took him on on a casual basis. He was paid each week and Rob gave Mrs. Jordan some for his lodging. He had suggested moving out, but they would have none of it. He was a help to them, for after work he would do odd jobs around the place.

"It's good to see you are a country boy, Rob," Peggy said one afternoon as they fetched in the herd for milking.

"Aye, it's something you don't forget. They were good memories," he answered.

"Have you forgotten all those bad memories yet?" she asked

directly. Rob was surprised at the question and its directness. "Well, it's plain to see that you've been badly hurt. I should think that's why you were on the road. But you're not a layabout, that's plain to see, so it's got to be something you're trying to forget or run away from."

"My, you're a wise one and no mistake," Rob laughed.

"And I reckon I could be wise enough for both of us, my lad," and reaching on tiptoe she turned to face him and pulled down his head so that their lips met in a tender kiss. At first Rob struggled and then as he got the feel and scent of her trim, firm body, he allowed himself to give in to the sensuous thrill of a woman.

Finally she pushed him away and smiling said, "There, that's better. A good old kiss and cuddle does the world of good."

"You done it before then?"

Smiling, she said, "No, not really. I've never loved anyone before you Rob."

"Love? That's a bit strong."

"Well, strong or not, it's the truth. I love you and if you won't act like a man then I'll come straight out with it and ask you to wed me. There you are, see, I knew you loved me as well," and again she kissed him. "Come on, we'd best tell father."

The words shocked Rob so much he began to tremble. He didn't know what to do. She was a lovely girl and no doubt if they married he would be set for life, part of a farm and, more than likely, the blacksmith's shop. It was very tempting. He did not love the girl, or at least he did love her, but not as he had loved Amy. Nobody could take the place of Amy and his heart still ached when he thought about her. But Peggy would make a good wife and a pretty one. He decided to let things ride and see what happened.

Abe and Jessie were delighted. They did not care about the past, only the future, and the happiness of Peggy. "We'll make it a Christmas wedding and we can join the two celebrations in one," said Jessie.

And so it all began. Rob was moved out to live in the blacksmith's house as it was not considered proper for the bride and groom to live under the same roof until they were married. He enjoyed it all and almost got caught up in the excitement as the wedding day drew nearer. A cottage had been let to them from the estate and Peggy and her mother busily cleaned and decorated and furniture was found from the village. But at the back of his mind, Rob knew it could not go on. On visits to Lowestoft he tried as best he could to write and trace Amy. He even wrote to Mary, but there was no reply. The worry lay heavy on him though he tried to hide it from Peggy.

"You've got nerves, wedding nerves. We'll soon put that right," she said.

She meant of course the honeymoon, for, being brought up in a Christian house meant no hanky panky before the wedding. It was a refreshing change for Rob after the wordly women he had known. He looked forward to the evenings when they would take leisurely walks through the long winding country lanes. The sweetness of her kisses and her innocence touched the very depths of his soul. If only, if only, his heart cried out, but the only answer was a cold still silence.

Two weeks before the wedding he was sent into Lowestoft for a new suit. "We'll treat you lad. You've got to look smart to get married," Abe told him.

Rob decided to visit the post office again hoping that there would be word from Mary. He stood at the counter waiting to be served when a hand fell heavily on his shoulder. "Can't do it boy, you know you can't." The familiar voice of Sergeant Craddock filled his ears.

"What the hell...?"

"Sonny got in touch. He's not too well and he said about you having this convenience address. I've been staying here for nearly two weeks. I thought I might catch you some time. I'm not going to make trouble for you boy. I warned you not to wed yon actress bitch, but you wouldn't listen. But you are going to listen this time. If you so much as dare to go near that church to wed again, I'll inform the police. It's bigamy Rob, bigamy. You'll go down for a long time on that one."

Rob knew that he was right. The old friends had a drink together and Rob gave a firm promise that he would put a stop to it all.

"That's all right lad, you'll not go back on your word."

"No, but I've got to do it my own way, Sarge."

Rob returned to the farm and showed off his suit. He looked at the friends who had adopted him as their family. They hadn't known him from Adam, but they had trusted him and now he was letting them down. The next morning he went to Bill's graveside and bid him farewell. Taking only the working clothes in which he stood, and a few pounds in his pocket, he made a neat parcel of all his clothes, placed the money he had saved in an old tin box and addressed the lot to Abe Jordan. In a leter to Abe he wrote, "I'm sorry about this master, but it's not a bit of good. I can't marry Peggy as much as I'd like to for I have a wife, somewhere. I wish I hadn't. You've been so kind and I hate myself for doing this, but I think too much of Peggy to bring dishonour and shame to her and the family whom I have come to love as my own. Rob Clamp."

He left the letter by the barn door where he had spent the first night and quietly, in the grey dawn, he crept away down the lane that led to Lowestoft. His heart ached as he looked across the fields. He was ashamed, tired of the burden of life and hating his very soul for what he had done. He should have spoken up right away and not let it go as far as this. He couldn't bear to think of Peggy when Abe told her. In fact he couldn't bear to think of any of them.

At Lowestoft he went to the docks and sat on a wooden ledge looking down into the grey sea. The thought came that he should get right away from it all and out of the country. He stood up, shook himself down and walked towards the dock gate. Stokers and engineers were always needed for trips. That was what he would do. He walked through the gates towards the first door he came to. It was a trawling company and after a few preliminary words explaining what he did, he signed on the *Golden Rose* as a stoker and went to meet the skipper.

"Where are we off to then?" he asked.

"The Icelandic waters mate, the bloody worst spot in the world."

But to Rob nothing could be worse than the ache in his heart at that moment.

CHAPTER 15

Rob's baptism at sea was horrific. The men were great once they realised that he was not trying to escape from anything and therefore out for an easy ride. The skipper was capable, civil and authoritative and it was a good ship. The only drawback was the crippling seasickness which filled every moment. It began on the first day as, stripped to the waist he shovelled away at the great chasms of boilers which kept the ship going. As his stomach retched and his bowels griped his insides, he thought of stopping the ship and getting off. He went up on deck, looked at the great rolling mass of water beneath him and threw up with such velocity he reckoned it would hit the mainland even though they were more than five miles out to sea!

"Is it always like this?" he asked.

"For some, not for others. You look like being one of the unlucky ones. Grub up."

The smell of grease and sizzling food nearly killed Rob and he just couldn't understand how, with an empty stomach, he could still throw up. He hated the food although the cook did his best, but the stench of stale cooking lingered around the ship. He hated the smell of the cold slimy fish, he hated the scales and the sight of the mens' hands as they almost froze in the deep cold, red raw and cracked and bleeding with the soreness of handling the fish. "This bugger should be a pound an ounce," he muttered. "By hell, you'll not get me on another trip." He cursed and endeared himself to the fishermens' hearts. At last here was a man who knew the terror and perils of the sea, but they could not resist teasing him.

"You're a bright bugger. This is nought. It's a doddle. You should try the rough times, then you'd know."

"No I won't. I never want to see the sea again."

The trip lasted just over three weeks although it seemed more like three years. But Rob appreciated the comradeship and it reminded him of army life. Everyone stuck together. They looked after one another. Cook made him light things, soups, dried bread or biscuit and Rob was grateful, but it was to no avail. They made him arrowroot for what they termed "Gut rot". It helped a bit but the man who docked back at Lowestoft was a broken man. As he set foot on firm land he almost fainted.

"Come and have a drink Rob." It was the skipper, and he guided him to a quayside pub. "You're not the type for this job. Why did you do it?"

Rob was silent. He had almost forgotten about Amy, Peggy and the army. Now it came back with a fierce reality.

"You don't have to tell me, it's none of my business, but I can see that you are a trained man. What is your trade?"

"Blacksmith. Army was my job but, well, that's all over now."

"Married?"

Rob sighed. "Don't know, I honestly don't know. What I do know is I wish I were dead," and he laid his head on his hands in despair.

"It can't be as bad as that. Tell you what, I'm from up north, near Hull. Come up with me on the night train. There's work up there and I can put in a good word for you. Come on, don't give in, give it a try."

He nodded his head in agreement. After all, what had he to lose? He had some money from the trip in his pocket, and pastures new where he could look around might be the making of him.

They had a meal which, surprisingly, he kept down, and he immediately felt better. They had a few drinks together and, with a bleary outlook, boarded the night train and slept soundly during the journey. It was the best sleep Rob had had for three weeks and he woke with a start as the engine drew to a halt.

"Come on mate, we're here, get a move on." Rob followed the skipper through the barrier and into the station. "I'm off home now. You go down to the pub, the *Mermaid*. You'll get a good meal and a bed for a bob or two. It's clean and they serve a good pint. It was taken over a few months ago and I've got to know them well. They're a bit of a theatrical couple, but all right. Tell them I sent you and I'll meet you there at ten in the morning and see about getting you a job You'll be all right there until you get set up."

They shook hands and Rob made his way as directed to the *Mermaid*. As he pushed open the door and made his way to the bar, the familiar smell of beer, food and bodies assailed him. The barmaid was bending over the bowl washing glasses and, without looking round, said, "Right my dearie, what can I get you?" Rob turned to stone as he recognised the voice and the stance. She turned round and he found himself looking into Amy's face. "You?" he stuttered.

She laughed in her old familiar way. "Yes, me. What did you reckon. Thought you'd killed me? Look who's here Jack. The hero, the bloody hero."

All the old feelings of love, hate and anger welled up inside Rob and then he winced as Jack stumbled through the door, his left leg bent and twisted as he walked, leaning heavily on a stick.

"You can look all right. I've got you to thank for this," and he waved his stick threateningly as Rob stood mesmerised.

Amy looked the same, a little older and heavily made up, but pretty much the same and here stood two men, one crippled for life and the other crippled inside and all because of her. Rob turned and looked at this woman, wanting to hate her, wanting to hurt her, but again his heart lurched as he thought of the times they had shared.

"Calm down Jack," said Amy. "He's a customer. We don't want to lose our licence do we. Have you been to see the kids, Rob? You remember our kids? Have you been to see them?"

"I haven't been back long. I might go down to Mary's in a week or two when I get straightened out."

"Mary's be buggered. They're in the Brixton Orphanage. Your Mary died and they took them off Sonny. He was that cut up, he couldn't manage them."

"What do you mean, why didn't they bring them to you?" Rob shouted.

"What, with him to handle? He was like a baby at first. No, they're best off where they are. It gives them a settled home."

Her tone and couldn't-care-less attitude angered him and the old Rob returned. With a sweeping gesture, he swiped the bottles and glasses from the bar top and with a shout of, "You bloody cow, you bloody cow," he ran into the darkened street and did not stop until he reached the railway station. Buying a single ticket to London, he leapt on the train just as it left the station. He sat down, breathing heavily. He was angry, sad and sickened with himself for not having given a thought to his bairns, nor to Mary and Sonny. It had been himself he had been thinking of, only himself, and now he was ashamed. He thought of his mother and father. Were they still alive? There was so much to think about and so much to do.

Arriving at his old stamping ground, he decided to go to the police station and find out where Sonny had got to. "He's a bit cut up, mate," he was told. "We couldn't do a thing with him after Mary died. He's got one of those little terraced houses down by the gas works. He doesn't go out much, can't get him interested in anything these days. They should have left the kids with him. It would have given him something to live for."

Rob didn't wait to hear the rest, but quickly made his way down the alleys and streets to the given address. He hammered on the door. "Hold on, hold on, give us a chance?" It was Sonny's voice but there was no welcome when the two friends came face to face. "She said you'd come back one day, like a bad penny. Where the hell have you been then?" was his greeting.

"I know I should have got in touch, but, well, I thought the kids, and you and Mary, would be better off without me."

"And what about how we felt then, what about me and Mary? She cried out for you Rob, many times. Where were you?" Sonny's voice trailed off and he burst into tears. Rob placed his arm across Sonny's shoulders and eased him through the door. "Look mate, let me come in. It ain't a bit of good us arguing. Come on, let's see what we can do?" Reluctantly Sonny opened the door and, leading the way into the tiny, spotless front room, pointed to a chair by the table. "Best sit yourself down. Mary wouldn't have turned you away."

"But you would, I know. I deserve that, but what happened Sonny? You know I wouldn't have stayed away if I had known anything was amiss."

Sonny appeared to crumble and leaned heavily against the table for support. Rob realised as they talked that his children were now four years old. Four years had gone by without them knowing their parents. He had thought Mary and Sonny would take their place and had never reckoned on Mary dying. "I know that right enough, but it was too quick for any of us to know," said Sonny.

Rob tried to bring Sonny back as he stood staring into space. "Heart attack?" Sonny shook his head. "No. Consumption, galloping consumption. It only took three weeks to kill her. You know how it is in a pub, Rob, with men spitting on the floor. No matter how many times you tell them or put notices up, they still do it and that's where the germs are. She'd clean it all up, disinfect the floor and the closets, but the germs were still there. She had gone a bit thin over the last six months or so and I kept telling her to go to the doctor, but she wouldn't hear of it. I was doing extra duties, wanted to get my stripes you see, and look what it's cost me. I came in one morning from night duty and she was gasping against the bar there, couldn't get her breath for coughing. I got her into the back parlour and sent for the doctor, but it was too late. He sent a swab away, but I knew what it was before he said anything. She had gone that grey colour and her bones were sticking through her back. She lingered for three weeks and then just slipped away. Of course they took the kids. Broke my heart that did and all and nigh broke them too, the poor little mites. But what with it being a pub and me on my own and what Mary died of, well what else could they do?"

"Did Amy know about it all then?"

"Can't honestly say. I reckon she did. I put the word around, but she never came by. I took Mary home to rest, Rob, back to her family, in the old churchyard. Your mother was pleased about that and your sister Daisy was a great comfort. God I miss Mary. I'd love to go and see her grave now and again. She was my life, my whole life."

"And the kids?" Rob asked.

"They're in the Brixton Orphanage. I go and see them every week, but it's a bit of an old dragon in charge. You have to make an appointment as she doesn't like her routine upset. Here, let's have a drink and a bite and I'll take you up to make an appointment for tomorrow. We told them all about you and what a fine soldier you were, but we never let on about anything else. They think their mother is dead."

They had a drink of tea and some thick slices of bread and dripping and then made their way to the tall, dour building that looked more like a prison than a place where children lived. Two large double doors led into a courtyard and two more double doors lay behind and shrouded the main building. The carts had driven deep ruts under the inner door and they were filled with muddy, murky water. "What the hell have I been doing in letting my kids come into this?" said Rob.

They knocked at a small glass window which was brusquely answered by a uniformed man saying, "Yes?"

"My name is Clamp. My kids are in here and I want to make an appointment to see them as soon as possible."

The man rustled through some papers and then disappeared through another door. On his return he snapped, "Tomorrow afternoon at three o'clock. You can visit for half an hour."

"You tell them I'm coming," shouted Rob. "Tell them their Dad's come home."

The following day, Rob really smartened himself up for the visit, borrowing one of Sonny's suits and treating himself to a new cap and neckerchief. His heart raced as he was allowed through the big door and he stood waiting to be allowed into the inner sanctum. It almost burst as he saw two little mites creeping along the cart tracks of the inner gates and racing towards him shouting, "Are you my daddy?"

Rob hugged his daughter and looked down at the solemn, brown haired little boy. "Yes, yes I am," he sobbed and bending to pick up Jack he felt him flinch with pain. "What's up son?" The boy looked afraid and began to whimper.

"Now then, don't be a cry-baby. I suppose you are Mr. Clamp?" said a tall, large-framed woman dressed in black as she came striding towards him.

"You suppose right," said Rob, sensing that something was wrong. There was a feeling of great fear in the place. "My son seems afraid. What's wrong.?"

"Oh, nothing that a little discipline won't put right. He must be taught that's all. He wets the bed and his bottom is a little sore."

As the boy backed away, Rob said quietly, "Show me son."

"It's nothing Mr. Clamp, I assure you," said the woman as she made to take Jack's hand.

"Show me son." Rob's voice was calm but determined and he reached out and gently took the braces from the boy's shoulders and dropped his course navy trousers to find a mass of tiny cuts which had turned septic through being wet.

His daughter looked up at him and said, "The wire mattress cuts into him Dad, but they wouldn't let him wear his pants or have a sheet."

"It's all right son, we'll get it seen to. Missus, I'm taking the kids. If you were a bloke I'd half kill you, but I'll say no more. The authorities will hear of this."

The woman spluttered, "You can't take the children unless they are properly discharged. You might not be a fit person."

"I'm as bloody fit as you are missus. These kids are mine and I'm taking them away from this hell hole." And as Rob swept them both into his arms he felt Jack wince as he carried him through the daunting gates and into the freedom of the streets. Rob put the boy down and straightened his ruffled hair. "It's all right now son. We'll go to Uncle Sonny's and get some stuff put on. Don't worry, you're not going back to that place."

Sonny could not believe the state of the lad. The criss-cross of the mesh had dug into the flesh and rusted with the wet of his urine to leave a smelling, rotting mass. "What kind of people do this to defenceless kids?" he said. Between them they bathed the soreness and, padding up the little lad in soft, torn sheets, placed him on his belly between blankets on a soft feather bed.

"Dad, what if I wee the bed?" Jack whimpered.

"Well, what if you do. We've put a rubber sheet on and we can soon change things. You'll soon stop all that now you're safe with me and Uncle Sonny."

Rob cried himself to sleep, ashamed of having let his children down and ashamed that he had allowed all this to happen for the love of a woman. Well, now was the time for him to put things right for the kids and right for Sonny, whom he had harmed as much as anyone. He decided to take them all home to Suffolk to stay with his mother. She would love the kids and Sonny could have a bit of a holiday and a chance to spend some time with his beloved Mary.

When Rob told them of his plans, Sonny's face broke into a smile. "By that would be grand." He laughed bitterly. "We look a right couple of buggers, Rob. Not like a few years ago, aye?"

Rob shook his head. "No, not like the old days. Nothing will be like that again. I've been well and truly through the mill, and so have you. We're both a bit battered now."

"Bloody maybe, bor, but not unbowed," said Sonny, using the familiar term that brought a lump to Rob's throat.

Rob wrote to his mother and they stayed in London for another week until Jack's sores were nearly all gone. They healed well but the scars they left would linger with Rob for a lifetime. With great excitement they boarded the train, the children dressed in new outfits proudly bought by their Uncle Sonny. They had settled down well and with the usual resilience of children had almost forgotten all the bad things. Almost, but not quite, for some nights they would wake up screaming and were clearly terrified by their memories.

As they approached the old cottage, Rob had to stop and compose himself. It was just the same, as if the clock had rolled back and he felt like the boy who had so cleverly run away intending to return in splendour and glory. But here he was, a failure, a broken man, bringing home his kids to his mother. But his mother was overjoyed to have the little ones around."I'll be glad to have them bor. They're family. I'm not as young as I was, but Daisy will help me out." Rob felt grateful and more settled in his mind now that he knew the children would be all right there.

After a meal of good old suet pudding, the two men visited Mary's grave in the evening twilight. Now it was Rob's turn to cry, but he couldn't. The tears dried in his throat and all he could manage was an unspoken plea for forgiveness. Sonny just crouched down and stroked the grass is if he was smoothing Mary's hair, something he had done so many times in the past. It seemed to put his mind at rest and he was almost happy as they called at the local pub for a pint.

On the way home they fell into the old familiar marching step and Sonny began to whistle some of the old tunes. Their arms began to swing and soon they were marching as of old, two soldiers, shoulder to shoulder, sticking by one another and seeing it through.

They passed the old school and from the cottage nearby a tall well-built man came towards them with hands outstretched. "Well, I'm blessed. If it ain't young Rob. How are you doing bor?"

Rob stared and slowly recognised Fatty Walls. "Well, I shouldn't like to haul you off the wire top now my lad." They laughed together and Sonny was introduced. They started recalling their old school pals; one or two had died of the dreaded consumption, most were married and soon the inevitable question came. "How about you, Rob? I did hear..."

"Well, you heard right, Fatty. I was wed and now I'm not, but I'll survive. I'm a tough old bird."

"Aye, I'll second that. You were always a tough bugger," laughed Fatty.

They lingered a long time, laughing, joking and sometimes serious. Rob was back in the playground, sliding away on his hobnailed boots. How could he ever have thought them to be hard times? They were the best. Even a soot boy would have been happier than he was now. "If only, if only," his heart said the words over and over again.

His father was drinking heavily and was confused at times and obviously causing his mother concern. She talked to Rob as if the time between the years had never been. "The doctor wants him to go to the asylum for treatment. I don't want to certify him, but if he doesn't alter there won't be any other way. See if you can get him to go in for a while. It would give me and Daisy a rest."

And he tried, but there was no sense to the man. Rob decided that the least he could do was to take charge and after talking with the vicar, arranged with the doctor to get the old man in for treatment. "I can't say I agree with your methods," the vicar said. But when asked if he could think of any alternative, agreed it was the only way.

Old Clamp was a cantankerous old devil and quite a handful if he had a mind to it.

On the day, Rob said, "Come on father, you and me will go for a pint or two and do the old rounds. We'll call at the manor, Top Farm and then the pub." The old man agreed quietly and Rob saw to it that he had plenty to drink. They set off for the manor, as arranged, where the squire was waiting to greet them. Several drinks later they left for Top Farm where, after several more pints, his father was well and truly drunk.

As they left the house, the small donkey cart was waiting in the yard. Father stopped as he spotted it. "I know what you're doing, you young varmint. I know what you're doing, you're putting me away." But, in spite of the strong words, he made no attempt to stop them loading him in the cart.

Stepping forward the doctor said, "I'll take him, Rob."

"No you won't. He's my father, I'll see to him." Rob brushed away the offered hand and, whipping above the donkey's head, hardly gave the doctor time to get inside before setting off at a fast gallop.

The asylum was a small clay building used mainly for lunatics who could not be handled at home. He sighed for his father who allowed himself to be led gently away into an anteroom. "You can see to him now, doctor. Don't worry, father, just do as they say and you'll be back afore you know it." The old man ignored him as if resigned to a forced cure for what he termed 'just enjoying himself'.

"It's for the best you know," the doctor said as he and Rob left. "The DTs were making him a danger to himself and everyone else."

"That's what they always say," agreed Rob, but in spite of all his father had been, in his heart he felt a traitor.

"I'll miss him all the same," Mother said as they sat together at the supper table.

"He wasn't all bad, nobody's all bad." Rob's head was heavy with the effort of the drinking and he needed to get out and be by himself. "I'm off for a walk. Don't bother yourself. I'm not going to get drunk, just to walk." Sonny offered to go with him, but Rob refused. "I need to be on my own to sort things out. It's been a funny old time lately what with one thing and another."

Rob wandered lazily down the dark lane and into the meadow where he used to hide. The stillness engulfed him in memory. The old tree was still there and he ran towards it. Tucking his lean body almost double, he managed to squeeze into the hollow. The tree wrapped itself around him with a comforting firmness and all the old familiar memories and feelings came rushing back. Looking out he could see Mary coming towards him; young Daisy and the squire's son; and, as the mists rolled over the uneven ground, they made pictures and there in the distance, he could have sworn he could see Amy, Amy and the kids as he had always imagined them.

But all too soon, the pictures faded into darkness. He was glad it was dark. No-one would see or hear him as he took a deep breath and, without control, sobbed into the momentary safety of the old hollow oak.

CHAPTER 16

Rob stayed in Suffolk for almost a month. Mother would not take any lodge money, but he and Sonny went to the village shop on most days and bought food. He helped out at the smithy on the odd day or two and the money kept him going. Sonny offered to help, but Rob always refused. However he did allow him to spoil the kids with clothes and some basic toy. He delighted in colouring the head of a top with chalks and then watch his childrens' delight as it spun like the colours of the rainbow. They blossomed in the country air and relaxed village life. Rob showed them his old playing fields, but forgot to mention his truancy, or the old tree.

But after a while all this did nothing to allay his restlessness. He wanted to be off again, to get back to the outside world. Mother said nothing, almost as if she was expecting him to go, and Sonny decided to stay on. "I'm all right here. I like being with the bairns and near Mary and all. You get off back and get some work. Here, take the house keys. You can shack up there until you make up your mind."

"And you mother," said Rob. "Will you manage? What about father? What's to do when he comes back?"

"Be off bor. You're no good here with your heart somewhere else. The little ones are fine with me. They keep me alive. And as for father, well we'll see, we'll see. Sonny can stop as long as he likes. We'll be all right bor, never fear."

Before leaving Rob tucked the children up in bed, telling them he was going to find work. "When I get turned round, I'll send for you and we'll all live together, like a proper family."

"Why can't we stop here? We're a proper family here with Gran and Uncle Sonny," Cora asked.

"I know, but, wouldn't you rather be with me in the town?"

For a minute they stared at him and then slowly shook their heads. "Nope. We like's it here matey," said Jack and Rob had to laugh at his use of the local dialect.

"OK then foreman, I'll be off. I'll write and send things for Gran. You be good now and write to me."

"Dad?" His son held out his arms and Rob hugged him tightly. "I only wet the bed twice since we bin here," he whispered. And Rob knew that they would be all right, no matter what happened.

And so, for the second time, Rob left home, but this time in the old donkey cart driven by Sonny as far as Ipswich. As they reached the edge of the town he stopped the cart and looked around at the old familiar landmarks pointing them out to Sonny.

"Don't come any further. Get off back. You look after yourself and the kids."

"Take this Rob. Now don't be daft. I'll feel better knowing you're not strapped," and Sonny pressed a crumpled five pound note into his hand.

The two friends looked at each other and then solemnly shook hands. Rob jumped down from the cart and, with a half wave and a turn, walked away clutching the money in his hand. As he heard the donkey trap drive away to Sonny's exasperated encouragement, Rob stifled an instinct to run after the cart. But he knew that no good was ever done by turning back. He had to go on to get work and try and settle down.

Walking through the streets he took in every familiar landmark of his youth and finally stood in front of the well polished front door. He raised his hand to rap the brass knob, but something stopped him and, in a hasty gesture, he turned to walk away.

"Not leaving without a drink, are you Corporal?" The raspy ring of Sergeant Craddock's voice brought a smile to Rob's face and turning he gripped the outstretched hand. "Where the hell have you been? No letters, nothing. What you been up to?" The questions tumbled out as the door opened and Mrs. Craddock rushed forward to greet him.

They talked into the small hours. They had so much to say and Rob had so much to tell them. "Stay here tonight lad, stay as long as you want."

Rob gladly accepted Mrs. Craddock's offer, but for one night only. He refused to go to the barracks, not trusting himself to cope with the feelings he knew would swamp his heart and mind.

That night they all went down to the pub and were greeted by a host of people he had long forgotten. The five pound note burned a hole in his pocket and soon he was buying drinks all round until it was gone. Within a short time Mrs. Craddock was helpless, but it took slightly longer for the old sergeant and Rob to get the same way. By ten o'clock, however, the three of them were singing away, rolling all over the place and finally landing in a heap in the doorway. The whole pub enjoyed the sound of the three slurred voices each trying to sing a different version of *Nelly Dean*, and the spectacle of the very sedate Mrs. Craddock letting her hair down in such a way.

Rob staggered to his feet and blearily looked down at his friends. "Come on missus, we'd better get you home." He bent down and fell over the sergeant's body.

"Bloody hell, you here and all. What you doing here?" asked the sergeant.

Rob shook his head. "Don't know. Reckon I've come to join up."

"Join the army, that's good that is," the sergeant laughed and then belched loudly as the doors opened on two young Salvation Army officers.

The young lieutenant made to step around the bodies, but the older, more experienced officer, held his arm. "These are the people who need us John. We must find out who they are and take them home."

Their enquiries were met with a stony silence. "Don't know who they are. Never seen 'em before," answered the landlord with a grin on his bewhiskered face. "Does nobody want to own them then?" the officers asked and again nobody came forward. It was now a joke with the landlord leading the way. "Well, fetch the cart. We'll just have to take them back to the hostel."

Two more Salvationists came and helped to pile the drunken bodies into the black cart which by now was full and they set off at a steady pace in front of the band, the flag and the marching, singing corps. Rob could feel the swing of the cart and from his eye corners could see the sergeant and his wife, but as to where he was he neither knew nor cared. His head was rolling and his stomach was retching. At the hostel they were unceremoniously turfed out and lined up, those who could stand, including Rob and the sergeant, but not Mrs. Craddock.

"Where the hell are we? Oh, I feel bad," murmured the sergeant. "Come on missus, up's a daisy," and between them they managed to get her to her feet and they joined the line. "Have we been arrested? Oh no, I'll get done for this." Sergeant Craddock was worried and therefore very relieved to find out that they were about to be given soup and cocoa by the Salvation Army. But the food revolted their stomachs and they pushed it away.

"What about the missus?" Rob asked.

"Well what about her?" and the sergeant looked at his wife who was sitting on a wooden bench, head down on her arms and snoring from the table top with enough noise to waken the dead.

"She sounds just like a bleedin' beehive. Shut her up," another inmate called, and Rob had to restrain the sergeant from stumbling across and hitting him.

"I'll have you know that this is my lady — er — lady wife," slurred the sergeant as he looked across at his wife.

"I wouldn't tell anyone if I were you mate," someone shouted and a chorus of laughter filled the room.

"Can't we go home?" Sergeant Craddock asked Rob.

"Can you walk and take her?" and the sergeant saw the reasoning behind Rob's logic and slumped down into his seat.

"I'd give my right arm for a bed and somewhere to put my head down," said Craddock and, as is by magic, a senior officer and his wife came to their bench and started to pray.

"Would you like a bed for the night brother?" they asked and in unison Rob and the sergeant nodded. "Have you no home? Well, don't say any more my dear. Is this your wife?" The sergeant nodded in agreement again. "And she is your mother?" Rob, in smiling devilment, agreed. "Then you've had no chance have you son," to which Rob shook his head pitifully.

"Do you wish to repent and to sign the pledge?"

"We'll do anything if you'll let us get some sleep" said Rob.

"Then we'll pray," and in soft voices the officers prayed and sang a hymn before leading them to a tiny cubicle containing three wooden bunks.

"What? Is this for all of us?" Rob asked as they were ushered in.

"Well, you are a family and it's the best we can do."

Gratefully they laid themselves and the missus down and all fell into a deep slumber without taking any further notice of the officers leaving the room.

The three of them awoke simultaneously as if a magic wand had been waved. "Wherever am I?" Mrs. Craddock asked.

The sergeant started to explain. "Well, love, it was like this ..." But the words were never finished for, with a big bang, as if the whole world was exploding inside their heads, the Salvation Army band and singers greeted them from beneath their window.

"Come along now. Have a cup of tea and we'll go on the march. You signed the pledge, and on your behalf too, my dear, and we are now going to tell the world," said the young officer and he stood over them as they gulped their tea. Mrs. Craddock was still in a bit of a stupor and of the opinion that she was dreaming and would soon waken up.

Meekly they followed the officer out of the building and down the yard where the procession stood waiting to set off. A whole corps of about one hundred, including the band, the flags and the converts, was lined up. The missus was now completely confused but Rob and the sergeant were beginning to see this as a great joke, especially on Mrs. Craddock, who would never live it down. The drums rolled and their heads split open as the singing of *Onward Christian Soldiers* began. Like two well trained soldiers, the sergerant and Rob straightened up, or tried to, and each with an arm under Mrs. Craddock, they tried to march.

"Can I help?" asked a sober looking cadet.

Rob shook his head. "No thanks mate. I wouldn't miss this for the world."

They followed the procession until they were in their own area and, as if by magic, the whole neighbourhood turned out to watch the scene. "Go to it missus, go on Rob, hold her up," the voices rang out in tune to the tambourines and as the procession made to stop outside the pub, Mrs. Craddock came swiftly to her senses.

"Craddock, what have you gone and done?" she shrieked and, pulling off her best ostrich feathered hat which had been pinned tightly to her head, she advanced on the sergeant, chasing him up the back alley that led to their house. Always game for a laugh, the sergeant made the best of it, but she wasn't joking and with jabs from her hat pin, he quickly ran ahead of her.

Rob could take no more and sitting on the kerbstone at the side of the road, he collapsed in hysterical laughter. It was just what he needed, maybe not at the Craddock's expense, but he was so glad it had happened this way. They would never hear the last of it from the missus, but she couldn't say much having got herself in such a state.

Some friends came to his side and invited Rob into the pub for another drink. He stood up and looked at the crumpled and stained suit he was wearing and he felt awful. Feeling that a drink would set him right agreed to join them.

As he went towards the door he felt a hand on his arm. "Don't give up that easily sir. It's just not worth it."

He looked into the face of a well-built woman, older than himself, and with a beauty that was stern but serene. "And have you got something that is worth it?" he asked sarcastically.

"Well, at least give it a try."

Something inside him came to life and he looked again at the woman dressed in full Salvation Army uniform. "And has it done anything for you then?" he asked.

She nodded. "It has given me life, real life."

"Then I'd better have a go," and he cheekily took her arm and made to follow the parade. "Are you an officer?"

She shook her head. "No, I come from the Lincolnshire Corps. I'm down here visiting my sister. She's an officer. I'm Lizzie Baker, widow."

"And I'm Rob Clamp and — and I'm buggered if I know."

"Well, let's see if we can find out then," came her answer.

And Rob felt sure that they would do just that. This woman looked as though she could take charge of anything and he certainly needed some help. He was a prime candidate for conversion.

CHAPTER 17

Rob never returned to the Craddock house. Lizzie took him back to her sister's, fitted him up with a suit from the stores kept for down and outs, and gave him dinner and tea. "Well, does that feel better?" she asked as he downed the last morsel of bread and butter pudding.

"Not half. I'll say this, whoever cooked that meal knew what they were about."

Her sister Maggie preened, but the brother-in-law just grunted. He wasn't a Salvationist and he didn't think much to a down and out being brought into his house and fed and clothed.

Lizzie looked at Rob and said, "That suit doesn't look bad, Rob. It belonged to Carter the blacksmith, a very respected man."

"That's funny. I'm a blacksmith by trade," said Rob.

Lizzie's face brightened as she murmured, "A tradesmen, eh? Well, that's nice."

At the evening meeting of the Salvation Army Rob refused to march with the corps, but he trundled along at their side. He was given a collection bag and, feeling a bit daft, jingled it in front of passers by.

"You really did sign the pledge then," Sergeant Craddock's voice boomed out from the crowd. Rob grinned. "You made a good recovery. Where's the missus?" Craddock, smiling broadly replied, "She's sleeping it off. Quietest day I've had in years."

They laughed and Craddock made to usher Rob inside the pub. Lizzie was there in an instant. "He's not going in there. He's signed the pledge."

Rob looked startled. Nobody had ever spoken to him like that before. "Hang on a minute, you ain't my keeper."

Craddock looked at the unlikely pair before him and smiled. "You listen to her, Rob. She's got a good head on her shoulders," and, patting Rob on the shoulder, he walked away.

"Come on Rob, there'll be supper in the hall. It'll be a good meal," and Lizzie took over.

Rob felt safe. It was good to have someone in charge. It was a bit like the army, so dutifully he followed and after a while he fell in step with the corps and marched in rhythm to the music. After supper Rob didn't quite know what was expected of him. He could hardly invite himself to stay and yet Lizzie made no indication that he was to go. As he sat with her family he found himself relating his whole story, his career, marriage and family.

As he finished she smiled and patted his knee. "That's all behind you now. Why not come back with me. I've got a nice little place. I'm sure we could find you a job, a craftsman like you. It would give you time to set yourself straight."

"You just mind what you're doing our Lizzie. You don't know him from Adam," her sister warned, but Lizzie took not one iota of notice.

"We'll go back tonight, on the ten o'clock train. We'll be back by morning, nice and fresh to start a new week."

"The tickets. I haven't any money left," said Rob.

Again she patted his arm. "Don't bother, I've got a bit."

And that was that. Rob and Lizzie, whom he had known less than twenty-four hours, caught the night train to Lincolnshire, a journey of more than six hours. At first they sat at opposite sides of the carriage but, as the train sped on its journey, he moved across to her side.

"Are you sure about this Lizzie? You don't know me, I don't know you. You might be letting yourself in for all sorts of things. And how are we going to live? Am I the lodger?" he pointedly asked the question.

Lizzie blushed bright red and then spoke with far more cheek than Rob would have given her credit for. "At first maybe. We'll see how things go."

"What about your religion? Doesn't that forbid, er, that sort of thing?" he emphasised the words.

Again she blushed. "Religion might, but who says I'm religious. I got into this after George died. It gave me strength, but I ain't soaked in it or anything like that."

This gave a new meaning to the whole affair. Rob wasn't sure that he fancied her and, anyway, she looked much older than him. "If it's not too rude, might I ask you how old you are Lizzie?"

"Aye, you can ask. I'm as old as my tongue and a little older than my teeth," she chanted, and he let the matter drop.

They arrivea in the country town of Stamford which was very much like Stowmarket, except that they had a different brogue. Everyone greeted Lizzie as they stood waiting for the bus to take them to the village of Sibsey. They were very friendly and smiled indulgently at another of Lizzie's lame ducks.

The cottage was quite large with four bedrooms, two kitchens and a front room, all spotlessly clean and smelling of the old familiar *Mansion* polish and *Sunlight* soap. "Get yourself busy and light that fire," she said and Rob did as he was bid and soon the kettle was boiling merrily away and the tea made. Ham came on the table and bread and milk which had been delivered and left on the cool tiles of the dairy shelf. Rob closed his eyes and leaned back on the coloured antimacassar draped over the back of the wooden spelled chair.

"You look at home Rob," she spoke softly.

"Do you know mor, I think I am, at least more at home than I've been for many a year."

The next day, without losing any time, Lizzie took him up to the big house and introduced him to the two maiden sisters and their bachelor brother who owned the village and the farm land. "Can you use a good handyman Miss Mary?" Lizzie asked the taller of the two. Both were dressed in severe black dresses with necklines so high that they almost disappeared into their hair.

"Well, yes we can. Is this another of your good deeds Lizzie?"

Lizzie shook her head. "No, not this one. This is a straight lodger that's looking for work. He's a smith by trade."

"Well, that's a coincidence. Old Barker's been taken bad and it doesn't look as if he'll be able to carry on for several months. I don't suppose you could?" Master Rupert, who looked all of eighty, looked questioningly at Rob.

Rob sighed. This was all too good to be true. "I could that sir." He doffed his capped head and instinctively stood to attention.

"Thank goodness for that then. What do you say girls?" Again Rob had to smother a smile, the girls being not a day under seventy. "Could you start now? The hunters desperately need shoeing and I would so love to ride."

Rob looked down at his suit and then at Lizzie who smiled and said, "Don't bother, I've still got some things. I'll set you up and if I know old Barker, he'll have some aprons lying around."

"You'd better go down and have a word with him first, but what is your name young man?"

"Rob Clamp sir. Ex-corporal of the Horse Guards division."

"Then welcome Corporal Clamp. I'm General Rupert Withers, also of the Guards."

The name rang a bell to Rob. "Withers, sir? Have you got a brother in the Horse Guards then?"

The old man looked startled. "Why no — yes — I mean there's

young Pip, Albert's boy. My brother was killed in the Crimean, but his son is in the regiment at Whitehall. Do you know him?"

"I once had the pleasure of meeting him, sir, and a real gent he was too. I'm pleased to be here." Rob touched his cap and with a delighted smile the General held out his hand in welcome.

As they made their way to the blacksmith's shop Rob said to Lizzie, "It's like a fairy tale all this." Smiling up at him she softly replied, "I reckon all this was destined." And Rob had to agree. But a few months later, he wondered just what his destiny was.

The life of the village was bliss. They went to market each week together and sometimes drove the three from the Manor in the ornate pony and trap. The first time Major Pip came home, they had a right old yarn which lasted well into the night. He listened intently as Rob told him about his life since he had first met him as a young lad running away from home. Rob enjoyed the Major's company and the visits became more frequent. It brought back memories as they talked of the army and with it returned the longing for the life he had loved. He was content enough now, in a way, but he knew in his heart of hearts that something was missing, and it wasn't just the children. He missed the thrill of what was just around the corner. Here, he knew every brick of every corner. Day in, day out, it was the same — safe. He was grateful to Lizzie, but he knew, as he finally brought himself to speak to the Major about Amy and all that had happened, that the longings for her were still there.

He never got drunk, but the Major had to be put to bed on several occasions. Rob got quite merry and it amused him that Lizzie couldn't complain too much because he had been in the company of the village gentry, and that gave her an edge and a bit of status.

He wrote to Sonny and his mother and mentioned to Lizzie that he would like the children to join him. Lizzie was a bit unsure. "Let's have them for a holiday first, Rob. We haven't got used to each other yet."

Rob took her meaning. In all the months he had lived with her, there had not been even the smallest suggestion of sex. She fed him like a king and he paid her lodge and had money to spare. The house was spotless and he had never been dressed like this before, except for his military uniform. He gardened, grew all the vegetables and felt a contentment he had not known for many a long year, if ever. He agreed to the holiday idea. The children were now at school and it might be a bit too much to ask Lizzie to take them on all at once.

When he got home one evening he found a special meal waiting. In the middle of the table stood a cake with one candle centred between hundreds-and-thousands sprinkled over the top. "What's all this then? Is it your birthday or something?"

Lizzie smiled coyly. "No, but it's a year, well almost a year, since we met. I know it's a bit early, but I thought if you were having the children for a holiday, we ought to celebrate while we were still alone."

Rob looked at her. She had on a flowered silk dress and, in spite of her heavy build, she was a fine looking woman. He had not seen anyone around the village or town who took his fancy, except perhaps the maid up at the manor who sat in front of them each Sunday in church. And Lizzie had been good to him, taking him on trust the way she had. After the celebration tea, he offered to help her wash up. He did this most nights, but she usually refused and told him to sit down and rest. Tonight she accepted and as they stood above the old yellow sink, she coyly brushed against him.

"We could have an early night if you want, Rob."

Rob wanted her desperately. He had not had a woman for far too long and his loins ached with desire, not for Lizzie necessarily, but for the closeness of a woman's body. But he was flustered and did not know whether to go into her room or wait for her to come to him. Lizzie took the lead and, appearing in a voluptuous white creation, crept in beside him and snuggled close.

He could not wait. Desire overtook all decency and precaution and soon Lizzie was naked and he was between her legs. It was over quickly and, rolling on his back, he kissed her tenderly. "Are you all right?" he asked.

"I'm fine, Rob, fine." And he had to admit that she gave the impression that it was as enjoyable to her as it had been to him. "We'll take my room tomorrow. The bed's bigger and that will be our room." The die was cast.

But Lizzie kept avoiding the subject of the childrens' holiday until he got exasperated and said, "I can't keep putting them off any longer mor. Are they coming or not? If not, I'll go down there and see them."

This startled Lizzie, for Rob had not shown any sign of temper or resistance before. "All right lovey, don't get vexed. I only cherish our being alone, that's all. I've never known anything like it before."

The children were put on the train and arrived late one Saturday night. Rob rushed towards them and stared at how much they had grown. Dutifully they kissed him and Lizzie and then followed quietly to the borrowed horse and trap for the journey home.

After supper they melted a little and began to ask questions. "Can I see the shop tomorrow Dad? Can we go out into the fields? Can we ride? Grandad lets us ride."

Their talk of his father reminded Rob that, with only the odd letter from Sonny who had sold up and gone to live with Rob's mother, he had forgotten that his father was at home again and still not drinking.

Lizzie smiled at the children and said, "Go steady, go steady. Your father's a busy man. We'll see what tomorrow brings." But Rob took them down to the shop and then to the manor. Everyone was very kind and although the children were still uneasy in Lizzie's presence, they seemed to enjoy themselves.

When they had gone back, Rob missed them and asked Lizzie if she thought they might come and live with them. "Not in our state, Rob. They can't come until we are wed," she replied firmly.

He had never thought of that and she was right. "Then we'd best get wed then."

Lizzie glowed with pleasure and lost no time in making the arrangements. Three weeks later, in the village church of Sibsey, at eight in the morning, Lizzie married Rob. The witnesses were the General and Miss Mary and Miss Margaret made a wedding breakfast up at the manor.

The ceremony passed in a dream for Rob. He thought of Amy, of Sonny and of his children. Something chilled his spine and told him that this was not right, but he could not stop the ceremony. As he heard the echo of his voice saying, "I will," a shudder ran down his body and legs. But it was too late.

In the weeks that followed, Lizzie kept putting off having the children with many excuses, but he was adamant and sent for them. After the first day he knew it had been the wrong decision. Lizzie did not like the children. Things came to a head when Jack wet the bed and Lizzie gave him a good hiding. Rob was livid and lost his temper with her. His wrath frightened her and she began to shout prayers over his head.

Rob gathered the children together. "Come on son, I'll put you to bed. You too Cora." As he washed them he realised that they had become skinny. "You getting plenty to eat then?"

They hung their heads and he had to force them to tell him that Lizzie said they were very poor and couldn't give them much. She also sent them out to play as soon as Rob had gone to work and they had to stay out all day. If it rained, they had to play in the shed.

Rob went wild. "Don't fret. I'll send you back to Granny in the morning."

That night, despite all Lizzie's pleas, Rob slept with the children in their room and the next morning he packed their few belongings and sent them down to his mother's. What a fool he had been. Lizzie didn't want anything that caused a bit of trouble. He was fine but she had not reckoned on kids. And he really couldn't blame her. But things were never the same again. The relationship was strained and she took delight at jibing him in public for the way he had been when they met. He wanted to get out of the mess, but didn't know how to do it until an opportunity presented itself in the way of a disaster. War was declared.

The Major came down on leave, knowing all that was going on in the War Office. He hinted to Rob that a bit of a do was likely and asked him if he would join the colours again.

"Would they have me, sir?" he asked, after telling of his discharge.

"Every man will be needed, especially trained men like yourself."

When the announcement was made, the village went to the church and the vicar, although decrying war, said that every able bodied man should volunteer. Rob could have kissed him and turning to Lizzie he said, "I'm off with the Major. We're leaving at six in the morning for London. It's only right that I should go." Leaning forward, he kissed her and, for the first time in months, they slept together that night.

News of the heroes departure spread through the small village and as the pony and trap left for Boston station, a crowd stood waving and shouting good luck. Lizzie, with her Salvation Army bonnet fixed squarely on her head, begain to sing *Onward Christian Soldiers* and the crowd joined in lustily.

Some of the younger men chased after the trap until they reached the main road. It was a rousing send off and it filled Rob's heart with that old feeling of expectancy.

"You'll write?" Lizzie called out after their disappearing figures.

Rob nodded, but he knew that nothing on earth would bring him back. This was goodbye. Rob was on his way again.

CHAPTER 18

It was a long and tedious journey with the hot August day burning its way through the crowded carriages until breathing and moving became so difficult that bodies twisted and turned trying to find a comfortable space. The two men had found a seat and fallen into a deep sleep for the last part of the journey. As soon as the train drew into Kings Cross, Rob could smell the city, the city he loved. Drawing a deep breath, he touched the Major's knee and whispered, "We're here sir."

The Major stretched and, standing up, took down his case and handed Rob the brown paper bag which Lizzie had packed. Rob had an urge to throw it away, but decided against the idea thinking that a change of underclothes might be very welcome before the morning.

They reported to the headquarters at Wellington Barracks and the Major explained about Rob. "Well, we can do with men like you, the old Ragged arsed militia boys. Come along with me and we'll see what the Commandant has to say." Rob laughed at the phrase and followed the RSM. He could not believe his luck when he found his old Colonel sitting behind the desk.

"Why it's Clamp isn't it? Glad to see you back."

"Thank you sir and congratulations sir." Rob touched his shoulders to indicate the red epaulettes now worn by the General.

"What have you been doing with yourself then lad?" and Rob smiled at the words. It was a long time since he had been a lad. He told of his escapades and made the General laugh. "Well, what can we do for you now?"

"I want to come back in, with the lads sir."

The General look dubious. "Well, I don't know about that Clamp, not in view of what happened. I know there's no record against you, but it was a bit of a strain you know."

Rob's heart sank. The General sighed and for what seemed like ages, he kept silent and then thumped the desk loudly. "I know, the old ASC. The Army Service Corps. They desperately need re-enforcing to get all the services down the lines. They need craftsmen like you Clamp. No army can run without them. I'll just give Teddy Vincent a call. He's the C.O., and he'll take you on my word."

Rob was pleased. He would have liked to go back with his old regiment, but anything was better than nothing. The call was made and he reported to the Aldershot barracks the next day. Before he knew what was happening, he was in uniform with two stripes on his arm. "You can keep your rank. We're getting a lot of tradesmen in who know nothing of army life and routine. You're just the man we need. Take over the smithy. We need the horses seeing to and all the gun carriages strengthening. They've got lots of new weapons to fight the Hun. We'll have him flattened in six weeks or before Christmas at least."

This was the general opinion, but Rob was not so sure. They were all treating it like a big game. The lads coming in were not given enough time, weapons or drill and wouldn't stand a chance if caught in a tight corner. But he kept his peace and did his own job well. He devised methods that not only strengthened the work, but got it done in half the time. Within two months he was made up to Sergeant. He never went out, but spent all his spare time in the mess. He could not trust himself to mix with the crowds.

And then the orders came that they were being shipped over to France, to go behind the lines until the first push was over and then to keep supplies and repairs running. Keep them on the move was the order of the day.

The crossing was as bad as Rob ever remembered at sea. He was sick and almost kissed the ground when they landed on the quayside. His corporal was a former London bus driver with the impressive name of Hubert Entwistle who could drive anything from a horse to a motorised vehicle. Rob found him to be a good lad and they enjoyed each other's company. They saw that everything was unloaded and then formed up and marched to a small deserted French village. In the distance they could hear the guns and the animals became restless. "We'd best stand with them tonight," said Rob. "We don't want them running off with all this stuff." And in silent whispers, as if the enemy all those miles away could hear them, they guarded through the night.

Early next morning they were on the march again, in a hurry now to reach the fighting troops who needed repairs and supplies. They began to sing as they marched but the laughter and voices ceased as they watched the bus loads of wounded go past to the field hospital. "Them's city buses, not our lot," Hubert called out to Rob and turning, Rob saw a fleet of London City buses with their own drivers still in city uniform, driving with such calm that you would have thought they were still driving through the streets of the capital.

"By, it does your heart good that does Sarge. The Hun'll not beat us while we've got blokes like that," Hubert shouted. Rob agreed but he felt a sadness in his heart.

They finally halted in a Belgian town that looked as if someone had taken a sweeping brush and swept all the houses and trees into great piles of rubble and dust. It startled Rob and his men. This was war, this was a battlefield and, judging by the look of the men sitting by the roadside camps, it was rough. Ragged arsed militia boys was a good description for them.

The detachment was detailed to a row of barns that were still half standing on the edge of the town. Rob left Hubert in charge and made towards headquarters. He marched smartly in spite of being tired knowing that this was what he had been trained for and there was no use in giving in. There was a queue at the headquarters and he stood in line chatting to the other NCOs who were waiting for orders. Hearing a sudden scream and cry, Rob looked towards the main doors of what had once been the old Town Hall. He saw a lad of not more than seventeen or eighteen being dragged out by two NCOs and escorted by two pale faced young officers. "What the hell are you doing with him?" Rob asked.

One of the men answered, "Going to shoot him I expect. He looks like a coward or deserter to me and that's what they do with them to teach others a lesson in case they turn yellow and run."

Rob gasped and as he watched the young lad struggle he could stand it no longer. Rushing forward he tackled the two sergeants and pulled them away. "Let him be, give the lad some dignity. Let him walk like a man. Here, come on son," and he stood the lad up and almost broke down as the lad clung to his arm and sobbed. "Come on lad, I'll walk with you. Have you no feelings you men. He's only a lad. Can't you let him off? This makes us into animals not British Soldiers." His voice was raised and he turned sharply as someone shouted the command to attention.

A tired looking old General came out of the building and waving his stick asked what was going on. "Bit of mutiny sir. This here sergeant says we're doing wrong to execute this cowardly deserter. Says we're not British."

The General looked at Rob. "And what if we let him off? What will the others think, will the rabble think they can do the same?"

"You could punish him sir," said Rob at attention.

"And what about you then. Can we punish you?"

Rob stiffened. "If it will set him free, yes sir."

"You're a very brave man sergeant. What's your name?" Rob answered in crisp clear tones. "Well then, Sergeant Clamp, you can take field punishment. Tie him to that wagon wheel, set it off and then leave him there until morning. He might feel differently then. Let the lad go. Give him seven days' hard labour, and I mean hard."

The lad made to walk over to Rob, but with a wink and a shake of the head Rob warned him off. He was steeling himself for the punishment. Making no resistance, he allowed himself to be tied to the wagon wheel, arms and legs sprawled out and each one tied to a spoke. The silence in the square was deafening and even overshadowed the distant roar of guns.

"Right, set it off." and with a whip, the horse set off at a gallop. Rob's head and legs felt every bump. The road was uneven and cobbled and laid with debris from the battle. On and on the wheel turned, gaining speed as the horse went unhindered down the road. He felt blood pouring into his eyes and mouth. His boot was wrenched from his foot leving the bare toes to take the punishment. But never once did he cry out, never once did he show pain. The ordeal ended abruptly when he heard a drawling voice call out and the wagon was drawn to a halt.

Two burly Australians came round to look at Rob. "What the hell? You a Hun then mate?" Rob shook his head, unable to speak. "He's a bloody British soldier. You deserted or something mate?" Again Rob shook his head. "Then we'd better let you down." And they cut the ropes that had torn Rob's wrists and ankles. For a while he could neither stand nor speak, and then he told them his story.

"Well, your lot are worse than the Jerries. And you're supposed to stop there until morning?" When Rob confirmed this, they plotted that he would spend the night with them in a makeshift camp and next morning would be driven back to the headquarters and tied to the wheel again just before reaching the town. "We'll take you back matey. It will give us a real thrill to do that." Being typical outback men, they made a meal and a drink and then tended to Rob's wounds laughing, "We don't want to do too much. It might give the game away."

Before dawn next morning, they set off, only stopping to bind Rob to the wheel. They drew up outside the great door of the headquarters and one of the Australians got down and hammered on the huge knocker. "You in there. We've brought you a present." Eventually two NCOs came out and immediately sent for the

General who calmly walked down to the cart. "Hmm. Stood the punishment well did you Clamp? Might make an officer of you yet." And, just as calmly, he walked back inside stopping only to order Rob to be cut down.

The funny side of the whole episode hit the Australians and they sat down and laughed until tears rolled down their cheeks. "You bloody British, you really take the biscuit." Rob stood up, still bloodied and cut and slowly wiped his face with a piece of cloth handed to him. He shook hands with the two men and thanked them for what they had done. He knew, as they did, that he might well have been dead had they not helped. "You come and see us any time matey, you're one of us," they shouted as they went off.

A soldier shouted to Rob, "The General wants to see you Clamp." Rob prepared himself for more trouble and was greatly relieved to find that the man was very amenable, to the extent of offering a cigarette, "The boy, sir, did he...?" asked Rob. The General shook his head saying, "That's none of your business." But Rob felt better. Anything was better than senseless killing.

Rob was ordered to go up to the front line as supplies and repairs were urgently needed. He was given a hearty breakfast and then a horse to get back to camp as quickly as possible. The real battlefield was horrendous with the stench of rotting bodies, the wet, the mud and the grey faces of men who had fought day and night for several weeks. But they set to work repairing and replenishing supplies until their bodies ached for rest and food.

"We've done this lot sir," Rob reported to a young Captain.

"Then go onto the left flank. There's a company there who need supplies and help desperately."

Rob's group formed again and made to fight their way through a sea of mud, heaving, pushing and shoving the horses and carts carrying the vital supplies. As they neared the trenches the fire became heavier. Machine guns split-splattered through the air and they dived for cover. Screams rent the air. "Help, for God's sake help." Rob made to go forward but was stopped by one of the battle veterans. "Leave them until dark, sarge. If you go out now you'll be target practice."

Rob waited for a while but could not stand the cries any longer. Straightening up as if on parade, he marched up and down along the tops of the trenches calling out stupid orders like, "Hold fast lads, stand firm," and then he would sing. They thought he had gone mad and tried to get him down, but he persisted and they let him be.

Rob was startled to hear another voice singing, "Here I be, here I buggery." The voice was pure Suffolk. "Who's that then?" he cried out.

"It's me bor, Fatty Wells."

The men had to hold Rob back as he made to dash across 'no-mans-land' to get his old school pal. "Sing to us bor, like we used to at home," said Fatty, his voice trailing into the rising mist of the muddy fields and echoing with an eeriness that shuddered the soul.

Rob almost broke down and then with a surge of spirit he straightened up and, marching up and down, just in case Fatty could see him, he sang, "Here I be, here I buggery, here I come from Fareham, my old woman got plenty like me, she knows how to rear 'em." As he sang his voice got stronger and soon rang out with an assurance he did not feel.

As dawn came over the muddy hillocks and shone like a pearl along the rows of wire, Rob called men to his side and they darted and weaved across the ground to avoid the hail of bullets. He stopped at the first body and made to lift it free from the tangled wire. "You'll not leave me bor?" whispered Fatty and Rob almost cried out as he saw the mangled body, twisted and caught on the vicious barbs. "No mate, I'll not leave you," replied Rob as he gently tried to free Fatty. But as a hail of bullets whizzed above their heads, Rob simply ripped Fatty free, closing his ears to the screams of pain.

Grabbing another soldier and tucking one under each arm as if they were rag dolls, Rob ran like hell for the British trenches. With two men to pull along, Rob was unable to duck and it was only a miracle that he was not hit. He laid them down and turning to Fatty smiled. "Seems I'm always getting you off the wire don't I bor?" the Suffolk accent coming broad and thick. Fatty smiled back, "Well, I'm glad it was you bor anyway," and he fell into a deep coma.

Rob wanted to stay and see what happened to Fatty, but there was no time to lose and they had to move immediately to take essential supplies and cope with all the trouble on the right flank. The work was finally done and they were sent back for more supplies. Feeling dog tired, they took their time on the return journey. They rested at night in the shelter of hedges and ditches.

On the move again, the rain came down incessantly and movement became a nightmare. Duckboards sank under the heavy weights and the column came to a standstill. "You hang on here. I'll take a mount and go and get help. We'll be here till Christmas at this rate," shouted Rob and taking a horse, he wiped it down and made to mount. With one leg over the back and the other in the stirrup he paused for a moment to look around. He knew nothing more until he awoke in a field hospital, bandaged from neck to hip. A piece of shrapnel had entered his spine and almost shattered his back.

"You're for Blighty sergeant," a voice said, and Rob smiled weakly. He could feel the splinters of bone grating as he tried to move. A nurse came forward, tipping a feeding cup to his mouth and offering him a drink of weak hot tea. "Don't move, here have a sip of this," she said softly.

"How long have I been here?"

"Only four days. We had to sedate you to move you, but you're going onto a hospital now and then back home."

The hospital was sparse and clean but the cries of the wounded and dying kept Rob awake and made him realise that war was futile. After breakfast one morning a deputation of officers and the matron marched into the ward.

"Sergeant Clamp?"

Rob nodded, wondering what was happening now.

"Congratulations man, you've been awarded the DCM for bravery." Rob looked at the officer and said, "What bravery?" The officer replied, "You saved two men from the wire, don't you remember?" Rob then laughed at the idea of being given a medal for rescuing Fatty Walls.

Rob was shipped back to Britain and after a year of treatment in hospital was allowed home on leave on the understanding that he had constant care. Sonny came to the rescue and agreed to look after him. He was a hero, the war was over and Fatty was home, albeit a cripple, but he was alive and nobody within ten miles of the village was allowed to forget who had saved him.

Rob was still in constant pain and preferred to sit alone in the familiar fields than be hosted as a war hero. But he was on the mend although still confined to a wheelchair and Sonny would take him down to the meadow on fine days and leave him there. His children were quite grown up now and although they loved their dad, he had no real feeling of belonging to them. They were really Sonny's and his mother's. Even his sister Daisy did more for them than Rob did, but they were proud of him, and when arrangements were made for the Commanding Officer to come down to award Rob his medal, the whole village was in an uproar. Flags were put out, a tea in the school was planned and the vicar and the squire and anybody who was anybody would be there .

He felt embarrassed but glad in a way that his mother was still alive to see him do something to be proud of. His father had passed on during the war and now his mother lived with Sonny and the children in as much peace and comfort as she had ever known.

The presentation was to take place at the spot destined for the new war memorial if fine, or inside the church if it was raining. Rob hoped that it would stay fine and it did. Sonny proudly wheeled him to the spot, the band played and the school children paraded. His citation was read out in a loud clear tone by the Commanding Officer and his mother cried as Cora held tightly onto his hand.

The Commanding Officer stepped forward and Rob made to struggle to his feet. Fatty limped forward and whispered, "Here, I'll help you mate." So, with Sonny on one side and the crippled Fatty on the other, Sergeant Rob Clamp of the Army Service Corp stood to attention to receive his medal. The band struck up the *National Anthem* and tears rolled down Rob's face and Fatty sobbed. Rob could not help wondering if the cost would ever be counted worth it.

Rob returned to hospital just outside Hull for his final treatment, but it was six long years before he was well enough to be discharged. As he recovered, he suffered severe backache which nothing seemed to help. He wrote home to Sonny asking for his mother to give him an old recipe she used to make for his father after a hard day up the chimney stacks. Sonny replied with the ingredients listed and Rob got a visitor to take the recipe to a local chemist to have it made up and then three times a day he took two drops on a spoonful of sugar. The medical staff laughed at him, but after a month there was a distinct improvement and, against all the odds, he got stronger. Doctors who had said that he would never shoe another horse, had to admit his recovery was just short of a miracle. Rob retorted, "You don't know it all yet. My old mother could teach some of you a thing or two."

As the years had gone by, Rob had kept only in vague touch with Sonny and the children, but he had not heard of Lizzie since he had left for the war. On his discharge from hospital he decided to stay in the Hull area and with what little money he had left, he got lodgings with an elderly couple.

He never tried to see if Amy was still in the area and it was a great shock therefore when one night after answering a tap on the door his landlady announced that he had a visitor. It was his son who was now working at the seaside town of Bridlington, building the new sea front.

They looked each other up and down. There was a strong resemblance and no matter what anyone said of Amy, this was his son, although there was also a look of Amy in the smile and the tilt of the head. He was a fine boy and a son to be proud of, but there was no emotion. They chatted like two acquaintances who had met after a long absence, finding out about each other and trying to cover the lost years.

"Sonny give you my address then?"

Jack nodded. "I've also been to see mother, my mother. I didn't stay long though. She's in Bradford now. How about you Dad. What are you going to do?"

"Well, I've answered adverts in the paper, but nobody wants an old soldier like me."

"There's a bloke in Brid who's looking for a smith. I'm off back tonight. Come with me and try for it."

"You mean you want me with you? You don't know me."

"You're my dad ain't you?"

Rob laughed. "All right then bor. Let's go."

They caught the late train and Rob stayed with his son in clean lodgings up in the old town. He got the job and could hardly believe his luck when told to start the following Monday. He was thin, almost gaunt, but with a strength that said he could work. He would work hard and he had shown that he was a good smith.

Rob walked down the main road, aiming to go and tell Jack the good news, but somehow he wandered onto the sea front quite near the cliffs. He hated the water, but the cliffs looked beautiful as they hovered majestically above the rolling waves. He slid down the slipway and breathed the strong air. Across that sea men had died and he had been maimed to preserve this beauty.

His thoughts surprised him and then he felt the impulse to feel the coldness of the water. Taking off his socks and shoes he rolled up his trouser legs and waded into the sea. The coolness refreshed his tired feet and his spirits lifted as he watched the seagulls overhead. They swooped and dived, taking tasty morsels from the cliffs here and there and then, seeing that all was clear, nestled in a niche on the rock face.

He watched them intently for a while. They were just like him. He had swooped and dived all his life, flitted here and there — in search of what? Maybe his search would end here. Bridlington might be just the niche he had been looking for, his elusive haven.